THE
FALL
OF
GRACE

THE
FALL
OF
GRACE

AMY FELLNER DOMINY

DELACORTE PRESS

Text copyright © 2018 by Amy Fellner Dominy
Jacket art copyright © 2018 by Corey Jenkins/Getty Images

Visit us on the Web! GetUnderlined.com

Educators and librarians, for a variety of teaching tools, visit us at RHTeachersLibrarians.com

Library of Congress Cataloging-in-Publication Data
Name: Dominy, Amy Fellner, author.
Title: The fall of Grace / Amy Dominy.
Description: First edition. | New York : Delacorte Press, 2018. | Summary: "After a shocking secret about her mother is exposed and everyday life is turned upside down, Grace embarks on an adventure, searching for answers about her family's current situation. But she gets more than she bargained for when it turns out that she isn't the only one looking for clues." —Provided by publisher.
Identifiers: LCCN 2017001920 | ISBN 978-1-101-93623-8 (hc) | ISBN 978-1-101-93625-2 (el)
Subjects: | CYAC: Mothers and daughters—Fiction. | Secrets—Fiction. | Photography—Fiction. | Mystery and detective stories.
Classification: LCC PZ7.D71184 Fal 2018 | DDC [Fic]—dc23

The text of this book is set in 11-point Berling.
Interior design by Trish Parcell

Printed in the United States of America
10 9 8 7 6 5 4 3 2 1
First Edition

Random House Children's Books
supports the First Amendment and celebrates the right to read.

For Susan Fellner Schanerman.
My sister. My friend.

1

August

An awning stretches above the doors to the bus terminal, blocking the sun but doing nothing to stop the sweltering heat. It's a struggle to breathe, the hot air trapped and unmoving.

Like me.

Someone bumps my shoulder and I turn, tightening my hold on my backpack. But it's someone in a hurry who doesn't even stop. No one here knows who I am—I remind myself of this as my breath calms. I'm not breaking a law by being here. I've been "asked" to remain in Phoenix. I've been "cautioned" and "advised" and "strongly encouraged."

Not ordered.

My new hiking boots take me into the bus terminal. They're Salomons and not new at all. I bought them at Goodwill this morning. I would have been squeamish before—used shoes? Please. But now I congratulate myself on my ten-dollar find. The fitted black tee and dark green pants are my own—bought for a trip to Paris and made of breathable, movable fabric with pockets down the leg. I'm a long way from Paris, but they'll do. A white hooded jacket with wind protection is in the pack. It can get cold where I'm going, even in August.

The bus terminal is nicer than I expected. Clean and well lit. There are black mesh benches that run in a line down the center of the airy space where people are sitting, bags under their legs, and kids lying on their moms' laps. It's noisy the way it is at the airport—a wave of sound that conveys nothing but carries you along. The kind of noise you can disappear into.

Rhodeways Bus Company flashes from a huge neon sign. Departure times are listed on a blue screen below. Mine flickers near the bottom. DEPARTURE: 3:05 P.M.

I adjust the hat lower over my forehead. It's a seafoam-green ball cap with Mickey Mouse on the brim. I bought it on a birthday trip with Cecily two years ago. We were being idiots, wearing our mouse ears everywhere and waiting an hour for pictures with Tigger. The trip was a surprise from Mom—everything taken care of, including this hat. I am a thief in this hat. One more reminder, not that I need it.

If only my memories could be sold off like everything else.

I move through the main floor, hoping to outdistance

my thoughts. My bus will be leaving from the north end of the terminal and I head for the far bank of ticket windows. Out of habit, I scan the crowd, but no one recognizes me. I hardly recognize myself.

Grace Marie Pierce.

Even the name sounds like someone I used to know. A Golden Girl. The cherished face of the Family Fund and pure embodiment of the American dream: money, security, hope. A face that, in the past three months, has been spat on, slapped, and even one night, hit with a raw egg.

I fall into line at the first ticket window and take one more look around. The people who travel here do not travel in my world. There's a group of rowdy guys—most of them in ASU tees—tossing a Nerf football. A family is crowded on the far bench, the mother passing out sand-wiches wrapped in baggies like my mom used to do. A fig-ure in a blue hoodie and faded jeans is slouched against the wall. As I look, he turns away, the fabric of his hood completely blocking his face. I remind myself I'm not the only one with a reason to hide.

Maybe that man is looking for answers, too. Maybe he'll find what he wants at the end of his bus trip and maybe so will I. It's possible. Anything is possible. I shuffle forward.

Am I really allowing myself to hope? Am I really that stupid?

Then it's my turn. I speak into the grate at the bottom of the window. "One ticket to Ridgway, Colorado."

A man with tired eyes and sloped shoulders nods. "Round trip?"

I hesitate. I have to swallow before I can get the words out. "One way." I slide $187 in cash through the window.

Some things you don't come back from.

2

May

"Come help me choose!"

Cecily peeks her head out of my closet. "Have you narrowed it down to two?"

I look at the photos spread out on my bed. "Seven."

"That is not narrowing it down."

"I started with thirty." I wave at the rejects that are now scattered across the carpet.

"Keep going. Struggle is good for the soul."

"Struggle is not good for the friendship."

She blinks at me the way she does when she's pretending to think. "Yeah, nope. Two."

I stick out my tongue as she disappears into my closet. "I'm fairly certain there's a rule about saying 'Yeah, nope.'"

"Where's that black skirt of yours—the one with the diamond pattern?"

"You borrowed it and never returned it."

5

Her head peeks out again. "I did?"

"For the Valentine's dance at the club."

"Oh, no wonder. I blocked that night from my memory." She vanishes again. "I can't wear that to the golf banquet."

"Then give it back." I study the photos again. I've printed them out as eight-by-tens for the contest entry. I shift the images around on the duvet, arranging them in a different order. I love the one of the light shining from beneath a glass tray of Waterford stems—the halo effect around the base of the bowls is really cool. But . . . I toss it to the carpet. Wineglasses are probably not quite right for a national high school photo competition. "Six," I call to Cecily. "Now come help."

"Two!" Her voice is muffled. I wonder if she's into my shoes.

I shift to my knees, studying the photos at this new angle. "Why are you looking in my closet anyway? You have a million beautiful things."

"I know, but I love your million beautiful things better."

"It's a golf banquet," I remind her. "And the team sucked this year—including us."

"But it's a joint banquet, which means the boys will be there, which means Henry will be there."

"Henry? You cannot possibly be interested in Henry."

She appears again, blowing an errant strand of white-blond hair from in front of her eye. "Why not? He's gorgeous."

"Because he tells girls that he carries a big stick and it isn't in his golf bag."

6

She covers her mouth with a hand. "He said that?"

"To Marietta."

She disappears into the closet, but less than a second later she swings back out, a hopeful look on her face. "Do you think he's telling the truth?"

"Gross!" I cry, and toss a wadded-up tissue that doesn't come close to reaching her.

We both laugh as she returns to her closet shopping.

When Mom and I first talked about the idea of transferring to a public school this year, I hated it. Especially to Desert Sky, which is a terrible name for a school with a drug problem because everyone just calls it Sky High. But Cecily surprised me by wanting to transfer, too. *I'm tired of living in a fishbowl,* she'd said. I never thought her mother would agree, but her dad was up for reelection. Public school was just the right message for a congressman accused of being an elitist. (Which he is.) And it's turned out to be a great year. For Cecily, because of the boys. For me, because of Mr. Dean, who runs the photography department.

And because of the boys, too—one in particular.

"What are you going to wear?" she asks.

"I told Sadie I'd wear pants. She's worried she'll be the only one."

"Oh please. If she lost weight, her thighs wouldn't rub when she wears a dress."

"Don't be mean." I push the hair off my face, tangling my fingers in the length of it. "I can't think about the golf banquet now. It's two days away." The end of the school year is always crazy, but it's worse this year. I've got the banquet this week, plus junior prom on Saturday, plus papers in two classes and an oral presentation on *The Crucible* due next week. But none of that matters. Not like this photo.

Cecily comes out with my sapphire-blue sundress and holds it up in front of the full-length mirror attached to the door. "Why doesn't Mr. Dean pick the photo for you? He's the teacher. He knows better than you what might win."

"He says it's part of our maturity as photographers to evaluate our work objectively."

"Maturity is so overrated." She makes a face at her reflection and flounces back into the closet.

I'm tempted to agree. As part of Advanced Photography, everyone has to submit one photo—what we consider our best—to be entered into the National Foundation of the Arts Student Photography Contest. Every year thousands of entries are judged and the winners are recognized at a public show in New York City. I'm only a junior, so my odds of winning are roughly the same as being struck by an asteroid while holding a winning lottery ticket, but still. I want to win this thing. And lately . . . I scan my photos with a critical eye. I have a real chance.

I've always been drawn to beautiful things, but this year my focus has changed. I've started searching for beauty in what most people see as ugly. The way the inky line of an oil spill perfectly matches the soft white trail of clouds. A spiderweb, lit to a silvery glow. The spark of vibrant green where the sun breathes life on a weed between the cracks of a sidewalk. Even now, the work makes my pulse skip.

"They're all really good," Cecily says. She's looking over my shoulder. "You're definitely better than anyone else in our school."

Except maybe Sam Rivers.

Cecily holds up the blue dress and my new silver heels. "Can I borrow?"

"Not the shoes. I just got those for prom and I want to wear them before you stretch them out."

"Are you calling my feet fat?"

"I love your feet. I worship your feet. But they're not coming near my silver Valentinos. Now help me decide and I'll let you borrow the dress."

"You're holding a dress hostage?"

"Cecily, please."

She sighs dramatically and shakes back her hair like we used to practice in the mirror. We've been best friends since sixth grade, when her family moved in next door. By then I was already in love with photography and how you could freeze the world just the way you wanted it. Kids at school said I liked it because I could order people around. It's possible I took my role as class photographer a little too seriously, but I wanted to put my frame around everything. A few days after Cecily became my neighbor, I was experimenting with a new telephoto lens. Through the picture window of her kitchen, I saw more than I should have.

Maybe that's why I overlook Cecily's occasional cruelty. She comes by it honestly.

Since the two of us became friends, I've taken hundreds of pictures of Cecily. Hundreds of us together. I glance at the wall behind my bed. I started with a thumbtack and a photo of Mom and me, taken on the balcony of our place in Newport with a tripod and timer. Now that picture is surrounded by a collage of photos that covers nearly fifteen feet of wall. Some are shots I took for assignments or subjects that caught my eye. But most are memories. The wall is my history. Me. Mom. Cecily. Our group of friends. More recently, Gabe.

As Cecily sinks on the bed beside me, she points to the flat-screen that's mounted over my desk. "I've seen this episode before. The two mothers get in a hair-pulling fight."

I glance up. It's one of the wedding shows Cecily and I love—the volume is so low that I forgot it was even on. I dig the remote from under my discarded photos and hit the mute button.

She tilts her head and studies the prints. "God, I hate you."

"What?" I look at her. Her blue-green eyes are emphasized with eye pencil and lash extensions, not that she really needs them. She's one of those tall, willowy blondes who could be a bikini model if her father weren't a politician.

"They're all perfect. Exactly like your life."

"Shut up." But I have to fight my smile, because the eye doesn't lie and they are fairly perfect.

"What do you get if you win?" she asks.

"There's a cash prize, but I'm in it for the fame and glory."

"As if you need it."

"I'd like to be recognized for the pictures I take, not the pictures I'm in."

She points to the extreme close-up in the center. "Is that Gabe?"

My heart skips. I know it's silly to be giddy over a boy, but I can't help it. I don't want to help it. I love this feeling—the breathless possibility that comes with having a boy say he likes you and you saying the same thing back. Mom, of course, is horrified. She says giddiness is an affliction of the young. "I just took that last week," I tell Cecily.

"Before he kissed you," she teases, "or after?"

"If it was after, the shot would have been blurry—my hands were shaking too much."

We both laugh. It was just a few weeks ago that Gabe and I were assigned to photograph the school play. We'd always been flirty with each other, but it was different being flirty in the dark wings of a stage. We stood so close, the sound of my heartbeat drowned out the actors.

During final tech run, Gabe whispered that he liked me, and he had since the first day of school. I was glad for the darkness offstage because I was blushing like a sunburned tomato when I told him I liked him, too. "I'm going to do this," he said, "before I talk myself out of it." And then he leaned in and kissed me.

Neither of us had gotten a single decent shot that day.

The photo Cecily is pointing to I took a few days later using a macro lens. It captures the geometry of his face. The curve of his cheek. The answering curve of his blond lashes. The slope of his nose. "I love the shape of it," I say. "I love that it's Gabe." *I could very possibly love Gabe.*

"The lighting is really cool," Cecily agrees.

"This one, then?"

"I don't know." She flips her hair to her other shoulder. "The lunar eclipse is still a favorite."

"What if other kids submit the same thing?"

"But it's not the same perspective, right? I mean, you capture the leaves in the foreground, Grace. It's cool. You're so good with details." She sighs and the edge of the photo flutters. "You see things that I would completely miss."

"I just look for what's beautiful."

She tilts a photo toward her. "Is this one new, too?"

"Yeah." The image causes my breath to catch, which is what a good photo should do. It's of my mom, a quiet moment with her on the couch going through a stack of mail. As I watched, the sun hit one of the tall cutout windows and beamed yellow-gold over the silk of her hair. I focused the camera and said, "Mom." She looked over and I caught her with a bemused smile. An unguarded smile. As soon as I snapped it, I knew I'd captured something real. Janelle Pierce is so many things to so many people, but this shows the heart of the woman I know—the one only I get to call Mom.

"You're lucky," Cecily says in a quiet voice.

I reach for her hand and squeeze. "You know she thinks of you as her daughter, too."

"If only." She smiles wryly. "I say go for it."

I nod. The decision feels right. "This is the one I'm going to submit." I brush the others aside, and before I can change my mind, I get the manila envelope Mr. Dean passed out last week. I slip the photo of Mom inside and seal it. Then I scramble off the bed and carefully slide the envelope into my backpack where it's leaning by the door. I'll turn it in tomorrow.

Happiness floods through me: relief that I've decided, and certainty that the photo is good. Maybe even really good.

Then, from behind me, I hear Cecily. "Grace!" There's a thread of fear in her voice. A chill runs down my back without my understanding why.

I turn to face her as she says, "Is that your mom on TV?"

3

August

The bus begins loading at 2:45 p.m. Since the route takes us through Las Vegas, I'm not surprised when the college guys, who already look half drunk, line up ahead of me. I'm careful to keep my eyes down. Mom always said my eyes are my best feature—honey brown with thick lashes. I've never seen it myself, always wishing I'd inherited her blue eyes and blond hair. My hair will lighten during the summer, but it's a definite brown, thick and wavy enough that I used to wear it in layers to my shoulder blades. But that's gone now, chopped off and lying on the bathroom floor that won't be mine in eight days.

I've been on buses like this before for class trips to California, and once to the Grand Canyon. The recirculated air is musty, but at least it's cool. I move down the aisle and find an empty row three-quarters of the way back. I slide to the window seat and set my backpack beside me, claiming the row for myself. Luckily, the bus isn't full. As I look out the window, only a few more people are heading this way. The family—the kids now sleeping over the shoulders of the adults—and the man in the blue hoodie.

The seat in front of me is empty and I stare at the back of it, hoping it stays that way. There's a stain on the blue-swirl fabric. Mud, maybe. Or blood. My right hand slides to the side pocket of my pants and the hard bulge of the knife. I don't know the first thing about using it, but if I have to, I will. Sometimes, like now, when every muscle is tight with nerves and the memories are pressing in, I want to use it even if I don't have to.

Exhaust pours from the bus, clouding my window. The terminal looks as if it's enveloped in a mist. It's almost magical, though I don't know what I expect to see. The doors flying open and Cecily running out? Gabe? Even if they knew I was here, they wouldn't care. I left a note for my uncle saying I'll be gone a few days, but he won't come looking for me either. I can't say I blame any of them.

"You look lonely."

I jerk, surprised at the voice. I'm expecting one of the frat boys, but when I turn it's an older man—about Uncle David's age. His smile is wide and makes my stomach turn.

"I'm not."

"You sure you wouldn't like some company? It's a long trip to Vegas—it would be nice to pass the time with someone."

"No thanks." I smile so I won't seem rude—a habit ingrained even now. His graying hair is combed back, and he has long sideburns. He's dressed conservatively. A logo on his shirt that I recognize and a belt around his jeans. Then I see the gap. The open zipper and the flash of what is very possibly skin and hair and things I do not want to see.

Seriously? I'm reminded of that game Mom bought on one of her retro kicks. A plastic camel that comes with a pile of sticks. Each turn, you add another stick to the camel's back until it finally buckles and everything spills off. I am that camel and the sticks keep piling on. Well, I'm done buckling. Disgust crawls up my spine as I raise my gaze to his. My hand slides to where the knife is. "Leave me alone," I say in a low but very clear voice.

"Everything all right back there?"

It's one of the college guys from the front of the bus. But I don't want any attention—I can't risk it unless I absolutely have to. "It's fine," I call back. My eyes stay focused on the man. It's a pathetic knife, the blade short and dull and meant to cut the foil off a wine bottle. But he can't know that with the blade tucked away. I slide it from my pocket and rest in on my thigh. The handle is shiny black and I let him see that I have it.

I'm breathing too fast—it's audible even over the engine of the bus—but I'm also ready. Maybe that's why he holds up his hands as he shuffles away, sliding into a seat at the rear.

Adrenaline kicks in then. A surge racing through my

blood and raising goose bumps along my skin. I just threatened a man with a knife. Three months ago, I hardly ever got angry. I never pushed or scratched or screamed or cursed. I never threw books or kicked tires or smashed a golf club on a tree. Now I'm carrying a knife, with everything I own in a pack next to me, and I'm alone on a bus on my way to somewhere I've never been. I let the thought sink in. Wait for the reaction that should come. The fear. The panic.

Huh.

I settle back, savoring what I've just realized. There's nothing left to fear when you have nothing left to lose.

The bus lurches, a belch of exhaust escapes, and then we're moving. Behind me the terminal fades and the bus bounces onto the road. Fifteen hours across four states. One transfer. Two stops. A drive. A climb. And then?

Then I'll know.

4

May

It is my mom on TV. At least, it's a picture of her float-ing at the top of the screen above a woman reporting . . . something. The TV is still on mute, and I stare from two feet away, wondering why my heart is hammering so hard.

My mom has been on TV hundreds of times. She's a mar-ket expert on local news shows, a guest on Sunday-morning financial programs. She's hosted charity events and given keynotes at high school and college graduations. It's the same picture she always sends when someone requests a PR photo. Her silvery-blond hair is clipped back, her gray-blue eyes penetrating and a little fierce. Her lips are closed but they hint at a smile. She's beautiful and she's a force of nature.

Then words begin to scroll across the screen.

LOCAL FINANCIAL MANAGER TARGETED
IN FBI INVESTIGATION.

The words make no sense. I wave a hand at Cecily. "Where's the remote? Turn up the volume."

"I can't find it."

She's behind me. I hear photos rustling, feel a pillow hit the back of my leg. I can't look away from the screen. The reporter is outside my mom's office building. I recognize the glass front, the metal beams that rise in a sharp series of X's.

ALLEGATIONS OF FRAUD

"I got it!" Cecily cries, and a second later the volume bursts on.

". . . after a tip that the office of a local investment firm was being visited by federal officials. As reported earlier, the target of the investigation is Janelle Pierce, manager of the Family Fund, who has long been a local success story and is well known for her involvement in the community."

"Oh my God," Cecily breathes.

I'm having trouble breathing at all.

The scene shifts and the reporter fills the screen. "The story took a startling turn as paramedics were called to the building. We're waiting on confirmation, but it's believed that Ms. Pierce was taken by ambulance to a local hospital."

"What?" I cry.

"We'll bring you more information as it becomes available."

I grab my cell from the bedside table. My fingers fumble

and the phone drops to the carpet. I scramble after it, hitting speed dial for Mom's cell, rising as it rings in my ear.

More words are scrolling across the TV.

INVESTMENT SCHEME UNCOVERED. FEDERAL

I squeeze my eyes shut and listen as the line rings two more times. Then the phone clicks to voice mail. "You've reached the phone of Janelle—" I stab at the red button to end the call. I was so sure she'd answer. That this is some kind of mistake. My lungs won't work. . . . I can't breathe against the pressure of my ribs.

The panicked disbelief I feel is mirrored in the paleness of Cecily's skin. "What do they mean, Grace? 'Investment scheme'? They can't mean the Family Fund, right? Not the Family Fund."

"I have to go down there."

"Down where?"

"Where they're taking her. The hospital."

"What hospital?"

I throw up my hands, tears hot and heavy on my lashes. "I don't know! I'll call Mom's receptionist. I'll—"

My phone rings. Hope spikes as I look at the screen. But instead of "Mom" I see a number I don't recognize. My hand shakes as I raise the phone. "Hello?"

"Grace, it's Barry Landry."

"Barry!" His name is a sharp exclamation of relief. Barry handles the marketing for my mom—he's the one who organizes all my photo shoots for year-end brochures and other mailings. "What's going on? I just saw something on TV. A reporter outside my mom's office. Is she okay? Do you know if my mom's okay?"

I hear him swallow on the other end of the line. "I was there," he says. "I happened to be there. At the office." His voice is rushed—shaky. "They had a warrant to search the premises."

I have to prop up my elbow with my other hand to keep the phone steady. "A warrant?" My eyes flash to Cecily's stricken face. "Why?"

"I don't know. There was evidence. Someone said the new accountant. I don't—"

"Barry," I snap. "I don't understand."

"They handed her a letter," he says. "She just . . . fainted."

"Who fainted?" I cry. "The accountant?"

"Your mom," he says. "They called the paramedics, and I got out of there."

"Where were they taking her?"

"Scottsdale. I called her lawyer, but I wanted you to know, too." Barry's voice drops an octave. "Look, I can't talk now, but don't say anything to anyone. Understand? Not a word."

Dread claws at my throat. "Barry—" But the call is already disconnected.

"Say anything about what?" Cecily asks. She steps closer, a hum of panic in her voice. "I could hear him through the phone, Grace. Don't say anything about what?"

5

August

I wake up in the dark to the feel of a hand clamped over my mouth.

I jerk automatically, struggling before I'm fully awake, before I even remember where I am. Then it comes to me with a rush. The vibration of the bus, the scratchy fabric of the seats beneath my back and legs. I must have curled my feet under when I fell asleep, and now I'm trapped beneath a weight. My cry is a muffled whimper under the suffocating press of a man's hand.

He leans down, his lips by my ear, his breath stinking of alcohol. "Shhh," he says. "I think you and me could be good friends."

It's the man from before. My arms are pinned beneath me and his knee digs into my thigh, holding me immobile. "Let's have a little fun," he says. "You know you want to." His shape is a dark blur as I whip my face, trying to break free. I whimper, fighting against my own helplessness.

And I thought I couldn't be afraid?

"Quiet," he hisses, "or I'll make you quiet."

"You going to make me quiet, too?"

The voice that comes from behind him is steady, almost bored. The man twists, startled. I react, yanking my hands free and shoving him off as I scramble back against the window. I can't see who's standing in the aisle—the man blocks him. My chest heaves for breath; my skin shudders as if I'm still being held. I pull my knees to my chest, trying to keep myself from flying into pieces.

"This isn't your business," the man says.

"Put your dick in your pants and sit down or I'll throw you off the bus myself."

"She wanted it. Her word against mine."

There's a soft sound of air and though I don't see anything happen, the man suddenly doubles over. His body jerks again, a second time, like a rag doll tossed off its feet. And then he's moving—being moved—to his seat. I lean forward until I get a glimpse of . . . blue hoodie?

It's the man in the blue hoodie.

Quickly, I tug my shirt down and with the heels of my hands I wipe at my eyes and my nose. Only now does my brain start working again, and it comes back to me.

The delay.

There was a mechanical issue, and instead of a short stop in Flagstaff, we were there for two hours. The daylight disappeared, along with everyone's good moods—except the college guys, who managed to get twice as drunk and twice as loud.

And now—I must have fallen asleep, rocked by the motion of the bus and my own exhaustion.

The sound of footsteps jars me into action and I straighten, blinking my eyes clear. I'm waiting with raised chin as Blue Hoodie makes his way closer. When he reaches my seat, I say, "Thank you so—" and then freeze as I see the man's face.

Not a man.

Not a stranger.

I know that wide, arrogant stance. The hard set of that jaw and the startling copper eyes that would be beautiful if they weren't so angry.

"Sam Rivers," I breathe.

"Hi, Grace," he says. "You taking a little trip?"

6

May

I've been to this hospital before. As soon as we come through the emergency room doors, I breathe in the memory of it along with the antiseptic smell. I squint against the too-bright lights, remembering those, too. I'm suddenly eleven again, and like then, I'm crying for my mom.

Please, God, let her be all right.

"Janelle Pierce," I say to the receptionist. "She's my mother. Paramedics brought her in."

The woman nods and scans a computer, adjusting a pair of readers. "She having some tests done right now, but let me find out where she's being taken next. If you'd like to have a seat for a moment?"

I look around. I don't want to sit in this room.

"Let me get you some coffee," Cecily says.

"What?" I blink at her, surprised by the offer. "I hate coffee."

"I know," she says. "But you're shivering."

Looking down, I see goose bumps on my bare arms. "Oh." I wrap my hands around my upper arms. My fingers feel icy. I should have grabbed a sweater to pull over the tank top and frayed shorts I wore to school. "I wish they'd brought her somewhere else. This is the same hospital where they brought me the night I got burned."

"Oh, right," she says. "The scars on your foot." She leads me to a row of chairs and sits me down beside her. "You were at a sleepover, right?"

"Josephine Shay's house." Cecily's heard the story before. The space heater. The quilt catching fire. Pain so bad I thought I was going to die. "I still remember Josephine's mom—we called her Miss Sylvie—running from the car to the hospital with me in her arms, bouncing me against these huge breasts and saying '*Je suis désolée*' over and over." I half laugh but it turns into a choked sob. I can't breathe. It's like I'm fighting that suffocating quilt all over again. "I just wanted my mom."

"She'll be okay," Cecily says. She threads her arm through mine and squeezes.

Though I don't tell Cecily this, the worst part about that night was that Mom didn't come. Not right away. Miss Sylvie called her over and over, for what felt like weeks and then years. In reality, it was three hours until she finally picked up her phone and came to get me. In the space of a lifetime, what is three hours? Nothing, really. Yet those hours—the awful feeling of being alone—sank into my bones and my tendons. It has grown with me, shaping me like a strand of DNA.

There's never been a father or sisters or brothers or godparents. I had a grandmother who died when I was four and an uncle I rarely see. A succession of babysitters were paid to care for me, but really there was only my mother. When she couldn't be found for those three hours, I refused to budge from that hospital room. Even then I was stubborn, and I knew I couldn't be without her. I never thought I'd be that afraid again in my life, and I never have been. Until this minute.

"Do you want me to call Ashley and Kendra? You know they'd come in a heartbeat."

I shake my head. "Not yet. Not until I know more."

"Grace Pierce?"

At the sound of my name, I shoot to my feet. The receptionist waves me over. "Your mom has been taken to ICU. Room 4B. Through those doors and follow the signs. Check in at the nurse's station."

"Should I come with you?" Cecily asks.

"Only if you want to keep your arm, because I'm not letting it go."

She pulls me close. *"Je suis désolée."*

7

May

The intensive care unit is on the fourth floor, and I have to announce myself through a phone system before the doors click open. Mom is being settled into a room—I stare down the halls wondering which one—while a nurse who introduced herself as Martina asks me a string of questions:

Did she have any symptoms?

Is she taking any medications?

Is she allergic to any medications?

Has she had any previous surgeries?

I have no answers. I can only shake my head uncertainly. It sickens me that I don't know these things about my own mother. Finally, I say, "Why aren't you asking her these questions?"

Martina has wide brown eyes and a face that makes me think of the expression "careworn." She's thin, in baggy blue scrubs, and there are lines of age and weariness etched in her dark skin. But her voice is so kind I have the urge to grab her hand. "Your mom was brought in by paramedics about an hour ago. She experienced strokelike symptoms and was unconscious and nonresponsive."

A sound escapes my throat. Cecily wraps her arm around me, her weight bearing mine as my knees go weak.

"Let me take you to her room," Martina says. "She should be settled by now." Her gaze shifts to Cecily. "You can come along, but just so you know, we only allow two visitors at a time in the ICU."

We follow Martina down a wide, brightly lit hallway. There are moaning sounds and mechanical beeps, and a man is whispering into a phone. Someone is sobbing. I focus on the squeak of Martina's rubber-soled shoes on the tile.

One squeak for every square.

Seventeen squeaks before she stops and I realize we're outside room 4B. At the threshold, I freeze. A man, also in scrubs, is bent over the bed, casting a shadow across a figure that's completely still. For a second, I feel a crazy rush of relief. It's been a mistake—this isn't Mom. Mom is never this still. Even when she sleeps, she's restless.

Then I see the freckle on the third finger of her right hand. A splash of brown on her center knuckle. When I was little, I would rub my thumb over it. She would ask, "What color do you think is under the brown?" And I would say *"Flamingo Pink!"* or *"Yellow Cake!"* I would guess and guess until I knew every color and the feel of her skin as well as I knew my own.

"Mom?" I whisper.

The doctor looks up. He's silver-haired with olive skin and dark eyes. Striking. Mom would like him.

She will *like him.*

"Grace, this is Dr. Ahrens," Martina says. "Your mom is in wonderful hands."

I nod, but I can't absorb it. There are so many machines. Lights flashing. Numbers beeping. As the doctor begins to speak, his voice is too smooth. I can't hold on to any of the words.

Left frontal lobe arterial bleed.

There's a tube in her mouth, tape holding it in place.

Blood in the brain tissue.

An IV in her left arm.

We intubated her to protect her airway.

Another IV threaded into her right wrist.

Blood pressure dangerously high.

"Grace," Cecily says, the urgency in her voice breaking through. I realize then that the doctor asked me a question.

"What?"

"Did she have high blood pressure?" he repeats.

I shrug. I feel so helpless. "I don't know. I don't think so."

"She might not have known herself."

"Is that what caused this?"

"It's difficult to be certain. But if your mother has high blood pressure, then a shock or a stressful incident could have created the perfect condition for the bleed."

His eyes flicker at the word *shock*.

Accused of fraud by the FBI. Is that what he's thinking? Has he seen the news?

"But she'll be okay, right?"

"Your mother is in a coma right now, which is not uncommon with a hemorrhagic stroke. We're going to keep monitoring and managing her blood pressure. Once we have her stabilized and the swelling in her brain goes down, we're hopeful for her recovery."

I accept the tissue that the nurse holds out. "How long until she wakes up?" I ask. "How long until she can talk?"

He purses his lips. "She might wake up in a day. Or a few days, perhaps. As far as speaking"—he sighs—"because of the location of the stroke, she may never speak again."

8

May

The first time I found God was on a beach in Mexico.

It was a dark night after a hot day, and the ocean was calm. The humid air tasted of salt. I was thirteen, and I was sitting on the sand with my camera when the water began to dance with tiny points of light. Green light. When I looked through my camera at the beauty of it, I couldn't imagine any explanation for it other than God.

I ran back to our casita and breathlessly told Mom. She was on the balcony, sipping wine and smoking one of her cigarettes. She laughed and called me a romantic. Mom has never been religious—she says anyone who lives their life by one book hasn't read enough. She explained that phosphorescence is caused by microscopic algae. I rolled my eyes at her. "You have to have faith," I said.

I keep thinking about that now, in this dim hospital room full of machines and bitter smells. With Mom's still form under two blankets because one seemed too thin to me. *"You have to have faith."*

And I do. I have faith in God and in the doctor and the nurses and in the goodness of the universe. But I want to tell Mom that more than anything, I have faith in *her.*

My fingers circle her hand, careful not to disturb any of the tubes. "You are the strongest person I know," I whisper into her skin. "You've always been a fighter, and now you need to fight this. Find a way. Right? Isn't that what you always tell me?"

Her eyes are closed, her face pale. Her blond hair is pushed back, the gray roots showing. Her skin, scrubbed free of makeup and powder, is spotted and uneven. This isn't "the lovely Janelle Pierce," as she's often called. "The woman who defies age as well as the markets." I want to shield her from everyone and say, "Don't look! This isn't my mom."

Instead, I cradle her hand in both of mine. I lean forward and put my head on her stomach. I used to sit with my head in her lap at night. I'd watch TV while she read journals or thumbed through paperwork. She always smelled so good. I search now for the floral scent of her French soap and tell myself it's still there. *It's still her.*

A shadow moves by the door. When I look up, a man is standing there: a stranger in a navy suit and a striped tie, with pale blue eyes that raise the hairs on the back of my neck. His gaze is fixed on Mom, and I shift in an effort to block his view.

"Do you mind?" I say.

He blinks and his gaze settles on me. Blue is a cool color—it's one of the first things you learn when you study photo filters and lighting. It's a color associated with calmness. A color meant to soothe. But his eyes . . . they're chilling.

"Get out," I say, an urgency I don't understand pushing me to find the nurse's button. But as quickly as he appeared, he turns and disappears.

Tension thrums through me, my body still on alert, as if it knows something I don't. I'm still staring at the door when Cecily walks in a minute later, carrying two hot chocolates. "Liquid sugar," she announces.

I force a smile, glad for the distraction. "Thanks!"

"Gabe is here," she adds.

My heart lifts. "Here?"

"You want him to come back?" She sets down the cups and licks a stain of chocolate on her hand. "I don't mind waiting out front."

I shake my head. I don't want anyone to see Mom like this. "No. I'll come out."

Cecily leads the way to the small waiting area outside the ICU doors. My heart thrums with a quiet happiness in the middle of all this fear. *Gabe is here.*

I find him sitting in the waiting area. His head is back against the wall, his long legs stretched in front of him. Belatedly, I smooth a hand over my hair and say, "Gabe, hi."

He turns to me, the expression on his face so strange my

steps falter. "Hey, Grace." Then he stands and I see that he's not alone on the bench.

"This is my dad," Gabe adds. His eyes shift, careful not to meet mine.

His dad? My training kicks in and I nod as he stands beside Gabe. "Hello, Mr. Woods." He's handsome—tall and blond. I see where Gabe gets his looks.

"How is your mother?" Mr. Woods asks.

"Not very good. She's had a stroke." I try to catch Gabe's eye, but he's got his hands stuffed in his jeans pockets and his gaze trained on a sign that says NO VISITORS AFTER 9:00 P.M. I feel like I'm missing something. Like I've turned on the TV in the middle of a movie.

Mr. Woods steps forward. "Well, we're very concerned. I realize this isn't the best time, but there are reports."

Gabe is still staring at the sign.

I look to Cecily and she asks the question for me. "What reports?"

"About the Family Fund." Mr. Woods hooks his thumbs in the pockets of his pressed khakis. "We've invested, along with many others in this community. Because of Gabe's connection to you, Grace, we recently increased our commitment."

Money? He's here because of money. My head is shaking and I can't seem to close my mouth. "I should get back," I finally manage, my voice cool. "Thank you for stopping by."

Mr. Woods's face blotches red. "You're her daughter. You must know something."

"Dad," Gabe mumbles. "Come on." He still won't look at me.

"I have to go," I say. Tears overflow my lashes and I blink hard in an effort to stop them. "My mother is in a coma." From the corner of my eye, I see someone standing behind me. Watching. Listening.

Anger flares when I recognize the suit and the pale blue eyes. "What are you doing here? Who are you?"

He's tall, with receding brown hair and a thin nose and lips. I expect his voice to be high, but it's deep, with a Boston accent. "Miss Pierce, my name is James Donovan. I'm a special agent with the FBI." He pulls a wallet from his coat pocket and flips it open, showing me a gold badge and his photo. "I was with your mother when she collapsed."

"Collapsed?" My trembling knees go rigid with fury. "You mean when she had a *stroke*! When you accused her of a crime she didn't commit and caused her to have a *stroke*!"

"I'm very sorry about her condition."

"Her *condition*?" I repeat. "Do you think she's faking it? Is that why you're here?"

He blinks, and even that movement feels precise and measured. "I'm just trying to do my job, Miss Pierce."

"Your job? Go away," I say, hating the hysterical shrill of my voice. "My mother is fighting for her life. You have no business being here!" A sob breaks loose, and then another. I'm aware of everyone watching: Cecily. Gabe. Mr. Woods. The strangers in the waiting area. The nurse behind the window. I can't make the noises stop. My vision blurs, my chest cramping as I hug myself, driving my nails into my upper arms to keep myself steady.

"I'm sorry," the agent says. "I'll be in touch, Miss Pierce."

"No," I manage. "I don't want you here. I don't want you anywhere near my mother."

"I know you don't want to hear this, especially right now, but your mother is the target of a federal investigation." He slips the badge back into his coat. "I will be in touch, and if you cooperate, things will go better for you."

My head wants to explode. "What will go better?"

"We have evidence that your mother was engaged in a scheme to defraud investors. We know you benefited," he says in an even voice. "There are those who will wonder if you also helped."

9

August

Sam Rivers. On my bus. I think I'm in shock.

He shouldn't be here. He graduated—was supposed to graduate—in May. If that's what it's called when you skip your senior year and take the GED. It was a huge risk, but Sam wouldn't care about that. It was obvious he saw school as a cage he couldn't wait to escape. Plus, he had plans. New York City. A photography program. And enough talent that he might actually make it.

If he didn't self-destruct.

Sam Rivers.

He hates me, like everyone else, but it's different with him. He's always hated me.

"What are you doing here?" I ask.

He lowers himself into the seat across the aisle. "The question is what are you doing here?"

My breath catches as I realize the obvious. "You followed me."

"Good thing, too." He sets a dusty black backpack on the seat beside him.

He's built like the football player he used to be, broad shouldered, and looks muscular even in a loose sweatshirt. He pushes back the hood and rubs his fingers over his scalp. His matted hair springs up, a dark brown that he wears a little too long. His eyebrows are a shade darker— thick slashes of emphasis around eyes that don't need any. Eyes that rise to lock with mine.

The muscles along my abdomen draw in. His eyes are always a shock. Light amber irises ringed by a deep brown. Tiger eyes.

The first time I saw Sam Rivers was in a photo taken at a gravesite. Cecily found it on the Internet beneath a headline that read *Tragic Funeral of Local High School Football Star.* Sam was fifteen, the article said. His seventeen-year-old brother, Marcus, was dead after an undisclosed accident. In the picture, Sam wore a white shirt, a blue tie, and a suit that was too small. He stood away from everyone else and his sadness bled off the screen. Of course he was sad, Cecily snapped, unmoved. It was a funeral.

But it was more than that. It was the tilt of his head that made him seem lost. The way his pant legs didn't quite reach his shoes so that I could see the tops of his socks. They weren't dress socks—they were white workout socks. I don't even know why I noticed that or why the image stayed with me. But it made me think of him long after the story had faded from the headlines. It made me want a wounded boy I didn't know to be okay.

I transferred to Desert Sky two years later. When I saw him that first day of school, I had no idea who he was. He wasn't a boy. And there was nothing wounded about him.

He strode into my advanced photography class like someone used to people moving out of his way. He took a seat in the back, and I couldn't help but follow him with my eyes.

In a new school, there were all kinds of boys to be labeled, and I'd seen a few who fell into the category of *Hottie*. This guy was more like *Damn*. Not handsome, exactly, but hard to look away from. Dark hair and those light eyes. As a photographer, I'd studied the geometry of faces. His was all sharp angles and shadows. Square jaw. Crooked nose. Skin that seemed stretched too tightly.

Everything about him seemed stretched too tightly.

Then it hit me. *Sam Rivers*. My breath caught on a silent gasp. He didn't look at all like the online photo, but somehow I knew that was who he was. I was still studying him, shocked, when he looked over and caught me staring. My face flushed so hot, I might as well have held up a poster with my thoughts: *Oh my God! You're him—the boy with the dead brother.*

Our gazes held and Sam's mouth twisted with something knowing . . . something self-mocking. I wanted to melt with embarrassment. But the strange thing—the confusing thing—is that I could swear in that first second he looked at me, his own eyes had widened in recognition.

But how could he know me?

As it turned out, that was just one more thing that didn't make sense about Sam. He was the unknown in a math equation I couldn't solve.

And I really hated unsolved problems.

Sam brought in photographs of roadkill and somehow made them look beautiful. He never seemed to pay attention in class, but when Mr. Dean called on him, he knew every answer. He was a jock who'd quit playing sports. A loner who could have been the most popular guy in school. And what was with the long sleeves every day? Why the heavy lace-up shoes? Did he work construction? Was that why he seemed so hard-baked? So much older than the rest of us?

Or did that come from having a dead brother?

"You only like him because he doesn't like you," Cecily said, rolling her eyes at all my questions.

"I'm not twelve anymore," I said. "I'm sixteen. I like him because he's completely wrong for me."

She laughed, as I meant her to, but the truth was I didn't know how I felt about Sam. I'd never known anyone so intense before. He scared me and fascinated me at the same time.

Damaged goods. That's how Cecily described him.

I wonder if that's how she'd describe me now, too.

"You've been following me this whole time?" I ask.

"Depends on what you mean by 'whole time.'" He raises the window shade and ducks his head to look. Lights flicker weakly as we drive through a small, half-deserted town. He turns back to me. "Since you got on the bus? Since you left your house? Since May?"

"You've been following me since *May*?"

He shakes his head. "In May, I thought the reports were still rumors. Too many people had invested." He reaches for the hem of his sweatshirt and pulls it over his head. There's a flash of flat stomach, and then he tugs down a T-shirt and drops the hoodie over his pack. His eyes are shadowed with exhaustion and he looks thinner than the last time I saw him.

"Then we tried to get our money," he says. "That was in June. My mother and I met with the FBI and they told us we'd have to file a claim. They couldn't promise we'd recover any of our investment."

"I never told you to invest." But my voice falters because the truth is I told everyone who would listen that they should invest.

"Then it was July," he goes on. "And still nothing. No money. Bills piling up. My mom is freaking out and what can I do? How do I unfuck this up?" His lips curl in a smile that doesn't reach his eyes. "Then I see the stories about the money. At first it's only online, but then it's being reported on TV." The bus rocks over a rough patch of road and he grips the top of the seats, shifting to face me in one smooth motion. "That's when I started following you."

How did I not recognize him in the station? Even without seeing his face, how many times have I seen him alone at lunch, crouched in the shade of a wall, his weight balanced on the balls of his feet so even at rest he's wound tight. Ready to bolt if anyone gets close.

He seems like that now, with his shoe vibrating in the aisle, his fists clenching and unclenching. He radiates anger as palpable as heat. How, I don't know, because his stare is glacial.

"Did you think you were just going to leave town unnoticed?" he asks.

I shrug. "Why shouldn't I?"

"Because you're Grace Pierce, and you know what even the FBI can't figure out."

I give him what I hope is a look of bored contempt. "I don't know what you're talking about."

"I'm talking about forty-five million dollars."

"Just because it's on TV doesn't make it true."

A muscle in his jaw pulses. "The FBI thinks it's true."

"The money is gone, Sam. Spent. All of it."

"Can't be. The FBI tracks that, so don't bother lying. There's still money that's unaccounted for and you know it."

I would laugh if it weren't so tragic. We're both on a quest for something that doesn't exist. "Let me guess. You also think I know where it is?"

"Here's what I think." He shifts forward, his knees wide, his chest filling the aisle. "You sneak out of your house with nothing but a backpack. Walk a mile to a gas station, call a taxi, and drive to the downtown bus terminal. You hide your face under a hat and keep quiet even when you're being attacked." His narrowed eyes flicker over my head. "And you have an interesting new haircut."

My hand shoots to my hair and I realize I lost the hat sometime during the assault. The sheared edges are prickly under my fingers. But what sends chills up my bare neck is that he knows all my movements.

"You've lost your mind."

"No," he says. "I've lost every dime we had. I've lost my mother's retirement and our whole fucking future. But my mind . . . that I've still got."

A weary frustration rises with my breath and I slide forward, claiming my own space in the aisle, knocking his foot with mine. I've been pushed as far as I can go, and his hate doesn't scare me anymore. It's nothing compared to my own. "I'm sorry for everything you've lost. For every shitty thing that's happened." My voices trembles; I can't help it. "You have no idea just how sorry I am. But that's all I have for you. That's all there is. I'm. Sorry."

He shoves back against the pressure of my foot. The world narrows until it's just me and him, the air humming between us. "Sorry might work with other people, but not me."

"Oh, you'd be surprised," I say. "It doesn't work with anyone. But you're not following me. I won't let you."

Headlights flicker through the window, painting shadows across the angles of his face. There's something compelling about his features—even beautiful. But then again, diamonds are also beautiful, and they're cold and hard enough to cut glass. "How are you going to stop me?" he asks.

"It won't be hard. You have no idea where I'm going."

"You're right." His lips curve and a shiver runs up my spine. "Guess I'd better stay close."

10

May

"A scheme to defraud investors."

I twist from stomach to back, burying my face in the pillow. I can't escape the words.

"We know you benefited. There are those who will wonder if you also helped."

It's somewhere between late at night and very early in the morning. I'm in Mom's bed, pretending to sleep, but mostly I'm breathing in the scent of her soap and soaking her silk pillowcase with my tears.

There has to be an explanation. A former employee who was stealing from the company. Or maybe the new accountant—whoever Barry was talking about. Or maybe Mom was being blackmailed or pressured or . . . I press my hands over my eyes. There's a reason—there has to be. Uncle David was traveling for business yesterday, but he flies back to Phoenix today and he'll meet me at the hospital. He's already spoken with a lawyer. He said it's a good sign that Mom wasn't arrested. But he also said I should be prepared for it to get worse before it gets better.

My cell phone vibrates, rattling on the nightstand. I roll over to check the screen in case it's the hospital. I don't recognize the number. I answered the first dozen phone calls tonight, and now I'm sorry I did. Those voices are inside my head, too: reporters asking for comment on the rumors about the Family Fund, strangers yelling into the phone about their money. And Gabe's dad wasn't the only school parent who wanted answers.

"Grace, it's Mindy. We were in bio together last semester. Listen, my dad wanted me to call. . . ."

"Grace, it's Harrison. My parents are freaking out. Call me."

I give up on even the pretense of sleep. I turn on the light. It burns my tired eyes, but it's better than the dark. Only a few more weeks until school ends—I'll have to go in for my oral report and final exams, but the rest I can do from home while I look after Mom. Then we'll go somewhere for the summer: the condo in Newport or maybe somewhere even farther. A bungalow in the Maldives. Mom can rehab in the turquoise waters, and we'll both soak up enough sunlight to forget all this ever happened.

The only thing I really care about is my photo for the contest. I'm especially glad now that I chose the photo of

Mom. I need to submit it to Mr. Dean. Somehow I know—
I can feel—that I'll win. Once I turn it in, I'll go to the
hospital. I'll talk to whoever wants a statement, and I'll set
them straight while I do. I can imagine Mom nodding in
satisfaction at the thought.

Don't forget, you're the face of the Family Fund.

I didn't really understand at first. I mean, no one notices
the face on a prospectus or an annual report. I just liked
the part where I got to dress up and have my picture taken.
But then the Fund started doing really well and Mom became more visible in the community. People knew who she
was—and it became a thing that the girl on the marketing
materials was her daughter. That the fund was growing up
with me—both of us doing so well.

"Don't become a drug-addicted prostitute," Mom would
joke. *"It won't look good for the Fund."*

"Oh darn," I would say. *"There go all my plans."*

But the truth is, I was proud of the Family Fund. You
didn't need a million dollars to take advantage of the amazing returns. Mom catered to families and working-class
people, as well as the wealthy. She welcomed smaller investors, and when I enrolled at Desert Sky, she created a
special program to bundle everyone interested into larger
pools so they could all benefit. Families were securing their
futures thanks to my mom. Of course I wanted to promote
that. I was doing a good thing by telling everyone. *A good
thing.*

It's 7:15 a.m. when I ring the bell at Cecily's house.

Already it's a beautiful day with a postcard sky. It must be a sign from God—it wouldn't be this beautiful unless something good was going to happen.

I dip my head and wipe beneath my swollen eyes, suddenly wondering how I must look. Uncle David wanted me to stay at his house with Aunt Caroline and the twins last night. But at nine o'clock when visiting hours ended, I stopped home for a few things and found I couldn't leave.

My hair is still wet from the shower. I've pulled it into a ponytail without even running a comb through it first. I'm wearing an old University of Texas T-shirt of Mom's and baggy shorts that I slept in. I'll fix myself up before the hospital.

I ring the doorbell again and tilt my head, trying to see through the glass and wrought iron. I took a photo of Cecily through the door once. It had a nice distorted quality, but I ended up deleting it. It creeped me out to see her look like someone I didn't know.

Behind the glass, something moves, and when the door opens, Cecily's eyes widen in surprise. "Grace!" She's wearing white shorts and a silver wraparound top she bought when we were at the mall a week ago. Her hair is half straightened. It's strange to think of her getting ready for another day of school—a typical Tuesday—when normal feels a million miles away.

"Hey," I say.

"You okay? How's your mom?"

"Same, but I'm hoping she'll come out of it today. I'm going to the hospital soon, and I wondered if you'd do me a favor."

She steps closer, leaning one hip against the doorjamb, the door pulled close so we're more private. "Of course. What?"

"Will you turn this in to Mr. Dean?" I hold out the envelope.

"Your photo entry?"

"I know it's crazy to even be thinking about this now, but . . ." I shrug and half smile.

"It's a great pic of your mom."

My eyes fill. "Thanks."

I glance over her shoulder at the sound of her mom calling from the kitchen. "Cecily, who is it?"

She stiffens, then leans in toward me. "You should go. My mom and dad are both freaked about the news. The phone was ringing all night. Your mom has donated to Dad's campaigns before, so he feels connected to the—" She stops.

"What?"

"People are saying she's a thief."

"You know that isn't true!"

She wets her lips, worry clouding her eyes. "It's the Family Fund, Grace. My college fund—"

"You won't lose a dime," I say fiercely. "I promise."

"Cecily?" her mom calls again. This time I hear the *click* of Mrs. White's heels.

Then she's there, and the door is jerked open, revealing her bottle-blond hair and her angular, Botox-smooth face. Her mouth hardens the way it does when she's angry. "What are you doing here?"

"Hi, Mrs. White."

"How dare you show your face at my door! Do you have any idea the destruction your mother has caused?"

"Mom," Cecily says, her voice soft but pleading.

"My mom wouldn't steal. She's not that kind of person."

"Apparently she's exactly that kind of person."

The tears I've tried to hold in spill over. "She'll explain when she wakes up. She's in a coma, Mrs. White."

"Isn't that convenient. Now she doesn't have to answer questions."

Her words slap at me, and the look in her eyes says she'd like to do more. I've seen her hit Cecily twice. Once through the telephoto lens of my camera. Once when I was here and she smacked Cecily across the cheek hard enough to cut her lip. I didn't say anything. I was thirteen and shocked, and Cecily made me swear not to tell anyone.

"I better go," I say, my own eyes thanking Cecily for the photo that she's still holding. "I'll talk to you later."

"No," Mrs. White says. "You won't."

"Mom," Cecily murmurs.

"Trust me," Mrs. White says. "You want nothing to do with her." She lifts her arm and Cecily flinches. Then her mom's hand slides over Cecily's shoulder and squeezes gently. "You were always too good for her anyway." Cecily gazes at her mom, a look of disbelief blooming into an expression of hope.

Then the door slams shut.

11

August

The bus has been following a highway west for what feels like hours of dark. It's quiet but for the road noise. Even the college guys must be asleep or passed out. We skirted the city of Kingman, Arizona, and I found that if I went a little cross-eyed, I could see rainbows in the passing signs from fast food restaurants, strip malls, and billboards.

I've always loved the light, but I never thought much about it until I got into photography. It's one of those things you take for granted, but when you think about it, light is magic. It changes the way people see things. Perceive things. *Feel* things. I thought I was going to use light to paint the world.

I tilt my face to search for stars, but I can't see a single one. Nights like this used to scare me when I was little and afraid of the dark. I didn't want to close my eyes in case a monster appeared. Little did I know that the danger lies in what people hide from us in the light of day. The monsters we know.

The monsters we love.

This stretch of road is winding and narrow, lit only for seconds as the bus's headlights sweep over boulders and craggy hills. I've counted four so far. Four crosses along my side of the highway. Ghostly white markers for people who were on their way . . . somewhere. What's it like to die that way? To see it coming, head-on, and be unable to do anything but rush toward it?

I jerk, trembling, the way I do sometimes when I'm nearly asleep and I have a sense of falling.

"Nightmare?" Sam asks. He's still in his seat across the aisle, but his head is turned toward me, his eyes a dark glimmer. "Did your mother have nightmares?"

I close my eyes, but I hear him shift in his seat.

"I've wondered about that. My mom has them. She wakes up shaking. Crying."

I have nightmares, I could tell him.

"You know what she said when she came home from meeting your mother?"

My stomach tightens—I've heard these stories before, and my body knows to ready itself, to absorb the words like punches. I open my eyes and face him. I used to try to block out the angry voices, but now I want to know. "What did she say?"

"She liked your mom. Called her 'lovely.'" He makes air

quotes. "Then she said the Family Fund wasn't taking new investors, but Ms. Pierce was going to make an exception because of us. Because you and I were going to the same school. Because the two of them were single mothers, so our families had so much in common." His voice shakes with disgust. "My mom wrote a check for our entire savings, and she thanked me for telling her about the Family Fund."

In the dark, it's hard to see him clearly. Once, in class, Mr. Dean told me I need to bring more shadow into my photos. *"The light is beautiful,"* he said, *"but you need contrast."* Now I'm glad for the shadow.

"How much did you invest?" I ask.

"My mom was only able to pull together thirty thousand dollars, but your mom said if she could come up with an extra five, she'd make it happen. So my mom borrowed from my aunt. Thirty-five thousand dollars."

I think back to the photo of Sam at the funeral. The white ankle socks beneath pants he'd outgrown. How did a boy with no money for a suit or dress socks invest thirty-five thousand dollars?

Should I tell him about the photos I've imagined lately? Photos of myself, beautifully lit and artfully styled. My eyes open and lifeless. In one, I'm lying on the sheets of my mother's bed. In another, I'm on a chaise by the pool in the backyard. When my body is discovered, there are stories on TV. I've imagined those, too. Reporters with somber expressions and folded hands as they give their reports. There would be shock and a sense of guilt. *She was a good person,* they would say.

Or would they?

I lean my head against the window. Mom used to spend thirty-five thousand dollars on a new watch.

"So did she?" Sam presses. "Have nightmares?"

"What would you like me to say?"

"The truth."

My mind slips back to nights when I would look out my window and see her sitting on the back patio in her cream negligee, the tip of her cigarette a bright red in the dark.

And further back, to when I would wake up in the night and tiptoe in my footie pajamas to the door of my bedroom, drawn by the sound of a man's voice. By my mother's throaty laugh. A sound I never heard during the day.

And even further back. Climbing in beside her with Gigi, my stuffed giraffe, so careful not to wake her as I curled up in her big bed. And her voice, smooth with sleep and warm with a smile. *"Tell Gigi not to steal all the covers tonight."*

So many memories like so many pieces of a puzzle. I keep trying to fit them together, but I can't.

The truth.

I lift my gaze from the past to look Sam in the eyes. "My mother did not have nightmares. She slept six hours every night and woke up full of energy. But it's possible she has them now. No one can say for sure with a person in a coma. But then, you know about comas, don't you? Because of your brother."

He flinches.

I'm not sure where the words come from, but I've developed a knack in the past month of picking just the right ones. In English, Mrs. Kennedy told us that words are the bridges that bring together nations. But words are also like bricks. If you lay the right ones down, you can build a wall between yourself and the rest of the world.

Or between yourself and a boy you can't have along as a witness.

"Turn around in Vegas," I tell Sam. "Quit wasting your time."

His face hardens, the skin drawing tight around eyes so angry I'm the one who wants to flinch. "But we're having so much fun. Besides, I don't want to miss the next bus to Ridgway, Colorado."

I can't hide my startled gasp.

"What? You thought you were going to lose me in Vegas?"

That's exactly what I thought. "Were you standing right behind me at the ticket counter?"

"Close enough. And why," he asks conversationally, "did you only buy a one-way ticket? Planning to fly home? A private jet, maybe, after you pick up all that money?"

"Maybe I'm not going home," I say. "Maybe I'm going to fly off one of Colorado's mountaintops."

"If you need a push, you let me know."

"Go to hell, Sam."

His lips quirk. "Only if that's where you're going."

I rest my forehead against the cool glass and close my eyes. "I've already been."

12

May

I pull into the parking lot of the public library and find a spot in the back, guiding my car into the late-afternoon shade. This is where Gabe wanted to meet. I didn't ask why the library—I'm just glad he texted.

It feels like the first good thing in four days.

Is it really only Thursday? I turn off the car and flip open the visor mirror. The golf banquet must have been last night. I wonder if Cecily wore my dress. I wonder if her mother let her. I smooth my hair, spreading it over my shoulders. The deeper shades of brown will start to lighten in the next month or so—assuming I see the sun. It still feels warm from the flat iron. I double-check my makeup. Too much concealer. I rub it in, but the truth is I look like someone who hasn't been sleeping or eating.

Martina, who is now my favorite nurse, brings me soup from the hospital cafeteria. I'm so touched that I eat as much as I can. Yesterday, I tried to pay her and her hands flew up. For a second I thought I saw horror on her face. I assumed she must be thinking the things they were saying on TV.

Stolen money. Dirty money.

But she gently folded my fingers back over the ten-dollar bill and said, "It's only soup, Grace, and not very good soup, at that."

A car door slams and I jump in my seat, my heart jumping with me. I've begun to startle at loud noises. At the sound of footsteps. At the ringer of my phone. I rub at my elbow. This morning in the hospital parking lot something hit me, sharp and sudden. I cried out, and when I spun around, a woman with gray hair and red-rimmed eyes was facing me. At my feet lay a crumpled ball of paper.

An earnings statement for the Family Fund.

But there's no one behind me now. No one in the library parking lot other than a woman with a stack of books in one arm and her hand holding tight to a towheaded boy.

It's nice to be outside. It's the first time I've left the hospital before visiting hours ended, and though it's only been four days, I've forgotten how bright the sun can be. How good fresh air and warm asphalt smells. I could lie on the back of my car and nap right here.

I've never been so tired in my life.

I'm tired of doctors who don't come when they say they will or who have nothing to say when they do. I'm tired of scratchy blankets and nurse rotations and terrible food. Mostly, I'm tired of being afraid all the time. Afraid of every odd beep from one of the machines attached to my mom or of the hiss of the blood pressure cuff that I hear in my sleep. Of the sound of every passing footstep, wondering if it's the FBI.

The accusations follow me everywhere—even to Uncle David's house. I've been staying there at night, though it's a half-hour drive from home. Uncle David insisted, worried that it isn't safe for me alone since the FBI shuttered my mom's business. People are scared.

And angry.

And maybe dangerous.

Reporters have begun to show up at my uncle's house, holding annual reports with my face on the cover, asking if I knew my mother was a thief. It's been hard on my aunt Caroline especially—I knew that—but I was still shocked this morning when I interrupted a whispered conversation in the kitchen. I didn't hear most of what my aunt and uncle were saying, only the last part, when my aunt said she doesn't want the stain of fraud to rub off on the twins.

"I'm not stained," I said, surprising them at the door of the kitchen. I wanted to say more, but I was crying too hard. I left and I'm not going back. Uncle David came to the hospital a little while ago. He said *"I'm sorry"* and *"It's a struggle right now with the girls"* and *"I know you're innocent in all this,"* but he didn't say *"Come back."*

It's not as if I'm alone. I'm with Mom. It's the two of us,

the way it's always been. I know she's awake, somewhere inside herself. Her vitals are stabilizing and her eyes have fluttered open, though she hasn't actually regained consciousness. The doctor says it could happen any minute. I check my phone now. I know the hospital's number, and it'll show up on the screen even with the ringer off.

In the meantime, Gabe.

It's all I can do to walk at a normal pace into the library. It's noisy and crowded, with people at every computer station. Even the tutoring tables are full of kids studying for final exams. I'm looking for Gabe's wavy blond hair. The polo shirts he wears in Easter-egg colors. His lazy smile.

Where is he?

My vision wavers and I swallow against sudden dizziness. I didn't ask where he wanted to meet. Are there tables in the back? Maybe he's at a table in the back. I start that way, weaving past the computers and into the stacks. I walk through Memoir and past Biography and then—

My breath rushes out and I feel ten pounds lighter. I don't know why I want to cry except that I'm so happy. *He's here.*

He's sitting at a rectangular table stationed in a small open space between the stacks and two windows. The slanted afternoon sun brightens even the green-gray carpet.

"Hi," I say. I push back my hair, forgetting about how I wanted it to look good. How *I* wanted to look good.

He meets my gaze and I don't want to remember him at the hospital, but it floods back. I've tried to make sense of it, hoping it was Gabe's dad who made the whole thing so awful. The fact that Gabe is smiling now is such a relief. I've been so afraid that he wouldn't want to be around me . . . with me . . .

I blush as I rest my hands on the top of a chair. Are we going to hug? Are we huggers now? We're kissers. We've kissed. But it was only the one time, and that was before all this happened. I want to sit next to him so he can hold my hand under the table, because that's what I pictured on the drive over. Our hands clasped and resting on his thigh. Our shoulders touching.

He stands from his chair for a second—half out and half in—but he doesn't come around. "Hey."

So I slide into the chair across from him. There's a strip of red running over the bridge of his nose. "You got sunburned," I say.

He frowns and then nods, as if he's only just remembered. "Pictures for swim team."

"Oh, right." My fingers weave together and then part. "I was supposed to shoot the tennis team."

"Marlene is doing it."

"Right. Good." I swallow. I smile, but I'm not sure he sees, because when I glance up, he's looking down at his hands. There's a *crack* as he bends back one knuckle and then another. "I almost never miss a day of school and now I've missed most of a week."

"How is your mom?"

"Better. They moved her last night from ICU to one of

the hospital floors. She's stabilized and breathing on her own now. She'll wake up soon." I pause and wet my lips. "I really miss . . . everyone."

My gaze flickers up, catches his for a brief second, and then we both look down. My heart thumps hard and heavy. I want it to be like it was behind the curtains in the school auditorium. I want him to sigh into my neck so close that I can feel his lips smile on my skin.

"When are you coming back?" he asks.

"I don't know. Next week, maybe. I don't want to leave my mom alone." My voice is stilted like my words. "We don't have a lot of family. It's only my uncle David, and they aren't close."

"Is that where you're staying?"

"I was, but I think I'm just going to stay at the house. I'm at the hospital most of the time anyway." I twist a silver ring around my pinkie, my thumb rubbing over the ridges of a Celtic knot. I've been wearing it every day as a talisman. Circle of life or something like that. "So what else have I missed?"

"Uh. Not much." *Crack. Crack.*

His fingers are long and slender. They look like piano-playing fingers. Like fingers that could reach across the scarred wooden surface of this table and take my hand.

But they don't.

"So how did the photos for the play turn out?" I ask.

For a second our gazes connect again. I know he's remembering, too. It feels like the memory is here, hovering in the space between us. I want us to jump into it like one of the chalk drawings in *Mary Poppins* and magically land in the wings of the stage behind the heavy velvet curtain.

Crack. He shifts in his chair, looking over as if someone is browsing in the aisles beside us, but no one is. "They turned out good. I actually went back and took some photos of the tear-down."

"That's a cool idea."

"That's what Mr. Dean said. Only he used words like *creative stretch*."

"And organic use of process?"

He grins. "Exactly."

"Mr. Dean and his catchphrases."

"Yeah." He half laughs, but the sound dies and it's awkward again. "If you come back to school . . ." He pauses. *Crack.* "Most kids don't know what to think."

"They should think this is all going to blow over. They should think everyone is going to get their money."

"That's not what they're saying on TV." He squints, as if he's looking at me through a long lens. "They keep showing the cover of the marketing brochure. So it's your face on the screen."

"It's just a picture."

Crack. "My dad talked to the FBI. He gave testimony."

"Testimony?"

"Well, I don't know if that's what it's called. But they interviewed him and took copies of all his records."

His words strike low, and my abs tighten to absorb the

pain. "It's only been four days, Gabe. Your dad is wrong. Everyone is wrong. If she's guilty, don't you think they would have arrested her instead of handing her a letter? I mean, what does that even mean, a letter?"

His Adam's apple works up and down. "Yeah. I guess."

"Gabe." I reach a hand forward. "Come on. It's me. It's . . . I don't know." I stop myself before I say *us*.

"Hey, there you are."

I turn. Charlie McDowell is walking our way. I blink at the strange appearance of him with his gelled hair, frayed sneakers, and four braided bracelets. I stiffen as I realize he's not surprised to see me. Or Gabe.

"I said to wait," Gabe mutters.

"Yeah, I know." Charlie grins and pulls out the chair next to me. He sits down like we're in photography class, sliding low in the seat with one leg bent under the chair and the other stretched wide. "Hey, Grace."

"Hey, Charlie."

"So," he says. "Your moms. Dang." He stares wide-eyed at me the way he does in class when he cracks a joke and plays the room for a laugh. He'd make a good politician, Cecily likes to say.

I look back at Gabe. My eyes burn.

"Charlie," he mutters.

"Did she do what everyone is saying?" Charlie asks. He looks from Gabe to me. "What? Everyone is asking at school. You might as well get used to it." He straightens, pulling his leg in so he can lean close enough for me to smell his minty gum. "You can tell me. It's not like my family invested in

66

your mom's fund. I think it's kind of badass. Your mom's the target of an FBI investigation—I mean, that's TV shit. She's famous. *You're* famous."

"And you're an ass."

"Oh, come on," he says with a grin. "You might as well tell us. It's all going to come out."

"There's nothing to come out."

"That's what Bernie Madoff said, too, in the beginning. You've heard of him, right? The reporters are saying your mom is just like him, and that dude stole, like, billions."

"Jeez, Charlie."

"What?" he says, glancing at Gabe. "I looked it up. Dude got a sentence of a hundred and fifty years. They're going to have to go cryogenics and freeze his brain so he can serve all that time."

My tongue feels swollen and useless. I stand up, surprised when the chair hits the back of my legs. I turn in time to steady it. "I need to . . ." I swallow. "I should go."

"Did you give her the lens?" Charlie asks.

"Right." Gabe's ears turn red.

I look from Charlie to Gabe, wondering what I've missed. "What lens?"

"The fish-eye." Gabe pulls it out, the soft black cloth bag reminding me of the day I took the photos of his face. I left him the lens to experiment with.

Now I understand. This is why he wanted to meet. Why we're in the back of the library. Why he keeps looking around.

I take the lens, my chin high. "Thanks." I spin on my toes

and walk away, but I only make it down two rows of books before I stop and clutch my stomach. My heart is racing, my vision clouded with tears. I have to catch my breath before I can make it through the lobby.

"Bernie Madoff had a kid, too," I hear Charlie say. "Two sons. One went to prison. The other one hanged himself from the ceiling of his apartment."

13

May

"I'm leaving for the day," a voice says. "Thought I'd stop by on my way out."

I'm hovering on the edge of sleep and I don't want to wake up. I don't want to be in the hospital holding Mom's limp hand. I don't want it to be Martina's voice, because if she's leaving, then it's dark outside and I'll have to face another night on my own.

But it is Martina, and that means the nurse who has become something like a friend has made the trip up from ICU to Mom's new room on the sixth floor. I rouse myself, turning to give her a weak smile. The hallway is still bright as day and humming with voices, but in Mom's room it feels more like twilight—shadowed and quiet. Martina is an outline at the door, her blue scrubs dark as a shroud.

"Hi," I say.

"Hi." Martina steps inside, and it feels achingly good to *not* be alone.

"How is she?"

"Stabilized. But she still hasn't woken up. They want to move her to a long-term facility, but her platelets are too low and her clotting times are too high. Or maybe it's the other way around." I shrug as she walks to the other side of the bed. "The doctor is supposed to stop by in the morning.

"Grace," she says. Her voice is barely louder than a sigh. "You can't manage this all on your own." She adjusts the covers over Mom, and I wonder if she knows she's even doing it.

"My uncle will be back. Tomorrow, I mean. He stops by every morning." Martina reminds me of my kindergarten teacher, Miss Mary. Her eyes are kind and bracketed by laugh lines. Even her ponytail seems bouncy and optimistic. "You have such a nice smile," I say.

She gives me a puzzled look. "I wasn't actually smiling."

"I know. But I can tell."

She smiles now. "What about your friend? Why not call her?"

The monitors cast everything in a blue-green light, including Mom. "It's hard for Cecily," I say, "because of her parents. They won't want her to see me until the investigation is over. It's the same with my other friends." But I'm guessing about that, because Ashley and Kendra haven't texted since Monday night.

"Isn't there another family member you could call?"

I shake my head. The beeps and flashes of light speak

their own language. "No other family. My grandmother died when I was little, and my grandpa was never in the picture. I don't know who my father is, and I doubt he knows about me either. My mom always says she didn't want a husband. She just wanted me. That probably sounds awful," I admit.

"Not awful at all," she says softly.

"Neither is my mom." I squeeze her cold fingers, willing her to wake up. "She's not any of the things people are saying." Her eyelids look so fragile. Like paper. Like if she tried at all, she could open them.

Footsteps sound outside the door. I startle and twist my neck to look.

Striped tie. Flag lapel pin. Cool blue eyes. A knot forms in my throat and I stand. He's been here every day. I've seen him in the reception area. I've seen him talking to the nurses. Now I see him even when he's not here.

I stride to the door and kick at the doorstop. Donovan steps back but he doesn't leave. I shove at the door, fighting the slow-release mechanism until it clicks shut. My eyes feel huge as I face Martina. "She didn't do anything wrong. You don't know my mom, but there's no way she would ever steal from people. Everything she was doing was to make sure the business succeeded." The words flood out of me, a transfusion of truth. "She wanted . . . *wants* everyone to do well. *Everyone.* She says we're a tide and we rise together. It's one of her favorite lines. She's involved in at least twenty different charities—we're always going to

71

events. She's just . . . she's the best person I know, and she wouldn't. You have to believe me. She wouldn't!"

The lines by Martina's eyes deepen as she squeezes my upper arm with one hand. "I believe you."

I cover her hand with my own and press my fingers into hers. "Why won't she wake up?"

"Give it time."

"How much time?" Tears begin falling and my eyes are so swollen they hurt. I never used to cry. I didn't have any reason to. "I keep talking to her. I keep asking her to wake up. Doesn't she hear me? Doesn't she know I need her?"

"Of course she knows. And I'm sure she's trying to make her way back to you." Gently, she moves me toward my chair. "You know what you need?" she says. "What you and your mom both need?" She squats down beside me. "You need to get out of this hospital. Out of this pain and worry."

I wipe my eyes, wondering if I could have heard her right. "How?"

"Is there some place you've been that makes you happy? A place you can take her with your words and your memories?"

I shake my head, but I suddenly know. There is a place like that. Well, I've never actually been myself, but my eyes drift closed and I can see it clearly because Mom has described it so often.

Southwestern Colorado. A place where the trees are as tall as forever. Mom went there for the first time when she was in high school and fell in love with it. She went again when she was pregnant with me, and then every year or

72

two as I grew up. One year when I must have been about eight or nine, I pleaded with her to take me.

"I already have," she told me.

"When?" I snuggled against her on the couch, breathing in her perfumed soap and imported cigarettes.

"I carried you up there myself when I was pregnant."

"That doesn't count."

"But you haven't heard the whole story."

A story? I tucked my feet under my legs and nodded for her to go on.

"I had photos of you: ultrasound pictures still in my wallet that looked like smears of white on a black background. But it was you, and I was feeling very Mother Nature with the mountains all around and the lake impossibly blue. So on a whim, I buried one of those ultrasound pictures in the dirt and covered it with a pile of rocks."

"You did?" I sat up, bubbling with happiness. "Is it still there?"

"No." She smiled. "It was gone by the time I went back, not that it would have survived the snowstorms. But I had more than squiggly line pictures of you by then. I also had a special glass jar with me. I sealed a picture in the jar and covered it with an even bigger stack of rocks."

"Which picture?" I demanded.

"The one of you reading *Charlotte's Web* to Gigi the giraffe."

"You buried my picture? Like a treasure?" I was mesmerized by the thought.

"It's at the edge of a meadow, overlooking a lake. That's

where you are, right now. My favorite person, in my favorite place."

Over the years, I've looked up at the stars and thought about that. A mountain in southern Colorado. A place she called Blue Lakes. My mom carrying me with her.

Smiling now, I open my eyes and say, "It's a place called—" I blink at the empty space beside me and realize Martina is gone. The door is closed behind her. I shift closer to Mom and take her hand again.

"You know where," I say, and it feels like she's listening. I repeat the phrase she used every time she described it: "Half a step from heaven."

14

August

The bus exhales a groan and shudders to a stop at the Las Vegas terminal. It's still Thursday, but just for a few more minutes. The lights outside the window are nearly blinding in the dark. I stand, stretching the crick in my lower back. I want nothing more than to get off this bus, but I wait until the sleazebag has gone by and disappeared inside the terminal. I wish Sam would disappear, too.

I've had time to consider my options, and it makes no sense to lose him in Vegas. He knows I'm going to Colorado. I don't have enough money to buy a second ticket, and even if I did, I don't have the time. I'm supposed to be back in Phoenix by one p.m. on Sunday.

If I go back.

I have to lose Sam in Ridgway, but how? I sling my pack over my shoulder, and as soon as I'm in the aisle, he's right behind me. I feel the size of him. The strength. Sam is at least fifty pounds heavier than me and six inches taller. I never saw him play football—he quit after his freshman year—but he's still every inch an athlete. Gabe said they tried to get him back on the team but he wouldn't touch a ball after Marcus died.

He's a runner now—though not for the school. I see him in the neighborhood. He's hard to miss. He runs mornings, he runs after school, he runs when it's too hot for anyone to run and when it's so cold I can see his breath when I drive by.

I can't outrun him and I can't overpower him. I have to outthink him.

The bus station is bright and metallic. There are banks of slot machines flashing lights and noise. I ignore those and search the signs for one that will lead me to the vending machines. I haven't developed a taste for coffee, but my need for Diet Coke borders on addiction. I start that way, ignoring Sam. He follows so close I can hear the creak of his shoes. I pull single dollar bills free from the stash in my front pocket. I never used to think about where my money came from. Now it's all I can think about. *So much money.* For a while, I thought I would pay it back. But that was before I understood.

The machine swallows the bills with a mechanical whine and then spits out my bottle of Diet Coke. I twist the cap and its ridges sting my hand, but it doesn't budge. I take a breath, but before I can try again, Sam takes the bottle. With one easy twist, the cap is off.

"I didn't ask for your help," I snap.

"I wouldn't have helped if you'd asked."

He turns back to the machine for his own bottle of Coke. He's so cool. So untouchable. And after all this time, he still has a way of getting under my skin. I remember ranting to Ashley a few weeks into school. I'd presented a photo of a bee perched on the edge of a red blossom, and when Mr. Dean asked for comments, Sam called my photo burnt.

"What is that supposed to mean?" I asked.

"It means," he said, "that your subject is so overdone, it's burnt."

Mr. Dean followed that with a lecture on constructive criticism, but I was still seething as we walked to our next class.

"Ignore him," Ashley said.

"I don't get it. Why is he such an ass?"

"He didn't used to be," she told me. "You should have known him before, Grace. He was different." Her sigh was heavy with regret. "He was . . . one of the good ones."

But I was stinging from his criticism, and I told Ashley it was time for him to get over it. Yes, what happened to his brother—*whatever* had happened to his brother—was awful. But you couldn't lose yourself in grief just because something bad had happened before.

Now I have my own Before.

"How do you do it?" I ask Sam, and I realize I really want to know. His eyes are copper in this light, but dull, like old pennies. "How do you not care about anyone or anything?"

He takes a drink from his bottle and screws the cap back on. "That seems like a good question for your mother."

I ought to be ready for the barb, but I'm not. It catches me deep, ripping into wounds that will never heal. "You must really hate me," I say.

He looks away, shrugging. "I don't care one way or the other." His fingers twist the cap off and on. "I thought we just agreed on that."

"We never agreed on anything," I say. But my words are a shovel, digging up another memory I'd rather not have. "Except for gray," I add.

His mouth tightens and I know he remembers, too.

We were only a month or so into school last fall when Mr. Dean paired us for an assignment. By then, I was trying to ignore Sam, but beneath the surface of my skin, I always felt a hum of awareness when he was in the room. It frustrated me more than I wanted to admit. Why *him*? Granted, he was easy on the eyes, but dark and brooding had never been my thing. When I was a little kid, no one had to warn me not to play with matches. I wasn't interested.

Until Sam.

It wasn't logical, and I was a logical person. But I couldn't help wondering if Sam was playing a part. I'd been raised to play a part myself. I was the face of the Family Fund. Always happy and optimistic. Sometimes it was tiring, but it also made things easier. If you give people what they expect, they don't look any deeper. I became an expert at smiling, and Sam . . . well, maybe Sam became an expert at scowling. I wanted to believe that the boy from the funeral photo was still inside him . . . hiding behind his own mask.

When the names were read off in class, my breath caught. Everyone had submitted their favorite color, and based on that, groups were formed. We had to find and photograph our color in an unexpected way or place. Sam and I were the only ones who had chosen gray. Walking to where he sat, I cursed myself for not choosing blue or green. For not asking Ashley what color she had chosen, or better yet, Gabe.

But I was also excited.

Maybe this was my chance to see behind Sam's mask.

We'd taken our cameras into the hall and I'd let him lead the way outdoors. What could I say? How could I connect? Then I remembered what Mom had always told me before an event where I was expected to make small talk with investors: the best way to start a conversation is by finding common ground. Our assignment gave me a perfect opening.

"So," I asked. "Why gray?"

"Why not gray?" he said. He didn't bother slowing down.

I should have left it at that. But I was sure I could break through his shell. That was how I'd always been.

Confident. Smug. Certain I could shape the world exactly how I wanted. I quickened my step until I was beside him. "My mom always says gray is the interesting space between black and white," I explained. "So I guess . . . it's always felt like a color of possibility to me."

He stopped abruptly, facing me by a brick wall that housed the school's air-conditioning units. They rumbled and hissed like caged animals.

"You want to know why I chose gray?" His amber eyes met mine, and my pulse jumped. "Because when your heart stops and you're one breath away from dying, gray is the last color you see."

Even now, in the noisy bus station, I can hear the echo of those words. They shocked me the way he must have wanted them to. They hollowed out my stomach and made me hate him. He must have wanted that, too, I realize now.

Maybe I'm not the only one building walls with words.

There's a sudden burst of laughter and voices from the walkway behind us. I glance over to see a group of girls who don't look much older than me. One is in a wedding dress. Three others are wearing puffy-sleeved teal dresses that are so dated they must have come from eBay.

I can't shake the sound of their happiness. I can't look away from their smiles or the strappy silver heels the bridesmaids are wearing. I was going to wear shoes like that to prom. I was going to go with Cecily and the girls and dance with Gabe. Was that the last time I felt happy? That Saturday night in May when it seemed like everything was going to be okay after all?

When I ran to Cecily's house with my hopes held every bit as high as my dress and my silver shoes.

15

May

Cecily answers the door. I've showered and my hair is dry, but just barely. I couldn't wait to get over here. I've got one arm raised so I don't drag the garment bag with my dress. The silver heels are looped around one finger, sparkling in the porch light that's on even though it's not quite dark. "Surprise!" I say.

I know her mom will be pissed to see me, but Cecily will be as happy as I am. I'm expecting an *Ohmygawd!* followed by a grin and then quite possibly a huge hug that puts my dress in danger of permanent wrinkles.

Instead, Cecily stares, her eyes growing wider and then narrowing. "What are you doing here?"

I think about saying something funny, but my throat is suddenly choked with doubt. "Mom's eyes opened today. She's still in a coma, but she's responding to pain. She's going to be okay, CC." I find myself using a nickname I haven't called her since middle school. "I just . . . I wanted to be with you. To be with everyone." I wiggle the hanger. "The way we've been planning."

It's Saturday night, and junior prom starts in two hours. I think the two of us started planning this before the school year even started. One of the best parts of transferring to a big school was going to be a big prom. When we became friends with Kendra and Ashley, we all decided to go as a group. The boys could dance with us, if deemed worthy, but mostly we were going to break hearts with our beauty.

For me, the plan changed when I kissed Gabe. When he said, "You're going to be at prom, right? Can we meet up? Ditch our friends? Dance inappropriately?"

I smiled wide enough to sprain my cheekbones.

Who knows, maybe I'll still break his heart with my beauty. Or maybe his heart was broken like mine and we can start over.

Cecily holds up a hand to stop me. There are tears glistening in her eyes. "Are you kidding me? Grace." She says my name like I'm an idiot. Like I'm five years old and I've just put gum in my hair.

"What?"

There are footsteps and laughter. Ashley comes down the stairs, followed by Kendra.

"Holy hell," Kendra breathes as our eyes meet from across the wide entry.

"Are you kidding me?" Ashley adds, echoing Cecily.

Confused, I look at Cecily, but her expression is unreadable now. Hard.

Kendra strides to the door and Ashley follows. They got manis and pedis today the way we planned, and their hair and makeup are done, but they're still in shorts and tank tops. They stand behind Cecily. I force a smile and a "Hey, guys."

"What are you— What is *she* doing here?" Ashley asks, diamond-studded bobby pins twinkling through her red hair. She looks to Cecily for an answer as if she can't possibly speak to me directly. Kendra does the same, ready to let Cecily take the lead on this. Whatever *this* is.

"What's going on?" I demand, dread crawling over my skin like a hot rash.

"The report," Cecily says. "It came today."

"What report?"

"From the FBI. They're saying the money is gone."

Kendra pushes forward, managing to shake back her glossy black hair at the same time. "Everything our parents invested is gone. Stolen by your mother."

Blood rushes to my face and I sway, scraping my shoes against the doorjamb. "It can't be gone. It can't."

"Then where is it?" Kendra says. "Maybe you're holding it right now. How much did those shoes cost, Grace?"

I stare at the heels. I loved these shoes the second I saw them. They're a true silver, not silvery-gray like others. I don't remember how much they cost. I just gave the woman Mom's credit card.

"Were they eight hundred?" Ashley asks. "A thousand?"

"Come on, you guys," I say. "You know me. You know my mom! Cecily, she's been better to you than your own mother. Your own mother—"

There's a blur of motion as Cecily's hand flies up and I feel the slap of her fingers across my cheek.

The sting is sharp and sudden. I cry out. My hand moves to my face and my forgotten shoes thud against my shoulder. I don't really feel it—hardly register the pain in my cheek. My gaze locks with Cecily's and I'm frozen in shock. I see anger, but also pain. As if I've just betrayed her.

Oh God. Have I?

Her lips are thin—just like her mother's. "Go home, Grace. You're not welcome here." She slams the door so hard the frame shakes.

16

August

The bus to Colorado has a slightly different pattern of upholstery than the one to Vegas, but otherwise it looks the same and smells of the same recirculated air. I'm nervous, half expecting the man who attacked me to be on this bus, too. Sam surprises me by moving down the aisle to the very back, checking every row before returning to where I've claimed a seat. He doesn't say anything and neither do I, but I feel better.

He sits across the aisle again, setting down his pack. His sweatshirt is stuffed away and he's wearing a gray tee, its long sleeves pushed up his forearms. I've never seen him in short sleeves or a tank top. He even runs in long sleeves. Some kids say it's because he's a cutter and he wants to cover the marks. Others say the sleeves hide evidence of the drugs he shoots up in his car. He did sit there alone sometimes, in the backseat of an old blue sedan. We'd see him when we left the parking lot. And he has a habit of rubbing his upper right arm with the thumb of his left hand. Like a druggie needing his next fix.

But he also showed up for class every day. He was smart enough to set the curve for most tests in advanced photography and ambitious enough that Mr. Dean did a write-up on the school's photography blog titled "Sam Rivers: A Bold Plan for New York."

And then there were his photos.

How could he have no heart and still capture images that spoke to mine?

I keep thinking of a picture he brought in this past winter. It was an old man sitting on a park bench, but he seemed more like a ghost than a human. You can see the man, but you also see through him to the back of the bench. I had no idea what technique Sam used, but the photo had an eerie quality. The old man is looking right at us, but do we really see him? Why not? Why is he disappearing? These past few months, that photo has haunted me.

Am *I* disappearing?

Someone stops by my seat. I glance up at the face of a guy who looks not much older than I am. He smiles, his face friendly, his hair and clothes rumpled as if he's been traveling a while, too. He drops a small pack on the seat behind me and is hefting a duffel to the rack above when Sam says, "There's plenty of room to spread out."

The guy turns and Sam shifts, raising one muscled arm over the top of the seat. "My girlfriend and I like as much privacy as we can get."

"Your girlfriend?" He looks at Sam and then across the

aisle to me, but if it seems strange that we're not sharing a seat, he doesn't press the point. "Sure." He pulls down his bag and gives me a quick smile before moving.

Sam stands, shoulders as stiff as a protective wall, and watches the guy stow his things three rows back. I should mind, I know, but I don't. I don't want smiles or polite chats. I don't want to make friends or be a friend or flirt or fall in love. Right now those things feel more distant than the mountains we're heading for. Right now they feel lost to me forever.

Sam runs his fingers over his scalp and sighs. His hair always reminds me of maple syrup. The kind that's dark amber in the bottle but flashes with gold under the light. It's long now—too long—and adds to the impression that he's someone you don't want to mess with. As the last people board, he hovers by my seat like a guard. "You shouldn't be alone," he mutters.

"I'm fine. I have a knife."

He shoots me a look of disbelief. "You know how to use it?"

"No," I say. "Can I practice on you?"

He grabs his pack and before I realize what he's doing, he's sliding in next to me, taking over the aisle seat, though I've got one leg stretched across it. I have to scoot against the window to avoid being crushed.

I shove at his shirt, half missing his arm and getting his chest, which has less give than the hard seats. He smells like cinnamon and sweat and the strawberry hand soap from the bus station. He settles in, taking up all the space—and my breath. I don't want him here—not this close. "What are you doing?"

He wedges his pack under the seat and sits back, his knees wide, his right leg almost touching me. My pulse hammers beneath my jaw. "We've got eight hours to Colorado. Thought I would nap."

"Not next to me you aren't."

He folds his arms over his chest and yawns. "Keep the knife hidden," he says. "Or someone will use it on you."

He closes his eyes as if he can sleep. Me, I've got every muscle clenched tight so I don't come out of my skin. My heart is racing, and sweat tickles the back of my neck. I've gotten used to being on my own, and to have him close enough that the heat of his skin is sinking into my own . . . it's unsettling.

From under my lashes, I study his features. I remember the way I captured the curves of Gabe's face with my camera. Sam is more straight lines and sharp edges. One eyebrow is a shade higher than the other. His nose is crooked, his mouth an unforgiving line in his square-jawed face. As I watch, his left thumb rubs at his right arm the way I've seen him do so many times in class.

Is he a cutter?

A drug addict?

Does he play death games like they say his brother did?

Beneath his chin, there's a scar, puckered into the shape of a pale V. It reminds me of another photo he brought to class. A pretty girl with wide-set brown eyes. Running across her neck was a deep scar like a pink choker.

I turn away, resting my forehead against the window as more images flicker through my mind. They play across the glass like bits of movies spliced together.

Grandma, lying in an open coffin. Pink cheeks. Red lipstick. The cloying smell of flowers. My hand in Mom's. *"Don't squeeze so hard, Grace. I'm not going anywhere."*

Pink construction paper. A crayon drawing of Mom with long yellow hair and me with brown. Stick arms and legs, matching orange dresses. In block letters: MY BEST FRIEND. *"I framed it, Mommy, for your office."* Did the FBI find it during their search?

A big red bow. Mom cutting it as families cheered behind us at a newly designed park. Later, in the car, with my beautiful yellow dress smoothed over my knees . . . Mom sighing dramatically. *"Those children were monsters. I don't know why that woman didn't take her baby home. He screamed during the entire presentation."* Me asking *"Did I ever cry like that?"* though I already knew the answer— I just liked to hear her say it. *"You were a good baby, Gracey. Always. And you were a very good girl today. We're quite the team, aren't we?"*

I sigh, my breath fogging the window. The image is clouded. Were we only a good team because I was a good girl? Another question to burrow under my skin . . . to infect me with its poison.

There's a photo from that day in the park. One of the

newspapers covering the event snapped it just before Mom cut the ribbon. She was wearing a wide-brimmed hat, and she'd tipped her sunglasses down just enough for the photographer to capture a playful glint in her eyes. She liked that photo—I'm sure of it.

Except now I'm not sure of anything.

17

May

When I pull into the school parking lot on Monday morning, the sign is still up in front of the gym: WELCOME DESERT SKY JUNIOR PROM. My cheek begins to throb. A ghostly reminder of Saturday night.

Of Cecily's slap.

Of my complete naiveté in showing up as if nothing had changed.

I left Cecily's house hating her—hating them all. But I've had a lot of time to think in the past two days. I spent prom night at the hospital with Mom, anchored to her bed like it was a lifeboat. For a long while, I didn't do much but feel sorry for myself. But around dawn, I realized I'd been doing a lot of that for the past six days. I kept thinking this was happening to *me*. To Mom. I finally realized it was also happening to Cecily and Gabe and all my friends.

The FBI was telling them terrible things. No wonder

they were afraid. But I knew there was more than what the FBI was reporting. If the money was gone, then someone else could be to blame. And if Mom was somehow responsible, then the money was still there somewhere, though she might have moved it. She might have had to, for better returns. And if she'd gotten creative—invested in something risky or not exactly FDIC approved—she would have kept it quiet. But the money hadn't been stolen. My mother was not a thief.

Neither was I.

Saturday night, my friends had been angry. They didn't want to listen, but I should have made them. I should have gone home and put on my dress and my silver shoes and shown up to prom. I should have forced them to face me and talk through what was happening. They were scared. I got that. So was I.

But we could deal with it *together*.

So I'm here. At school. I already requested a packet of homework, but rather than just pick it up, I'll walk to the Coffee Cart like it's any other Monday. And Cecily and the girls will be there, hanging out by the far post the way we always do before the first bell rings. I know I can't fix this in fifteen minutes, but I can start. And I still have a lot of friends. Kids in my classes, the advanced photography group, the girls on the golf team. I'll make them listen. I'll make them understand.

The office is crowded and noisy, and I breathe in the chaos with a smile. It's so . . . normal.

Then the secretary looks up and her jaw literally drops. "Grace!"

The room is suddenly quiet. "Hi, Mrs. Joyce."

"You're here to pick up your homework?"

"And go to classes."

Her fingers grip the edge of her desk for a second, and then she pushes back on the wheels of her chair to the filing cabinet behind her. Does she remember doing the same thing when I gave her an investor's packet for the Family Fund? Her gaze sweeps the room as she rolls back to me with a thick envelope. I don't turn, but I can feel eyes on my back and it's all I can do not to flinch. I steel myself for Mrs. Joyce's anger when she hands me my packet, but when our eyes meet, I see her concern . . . and I see that it's for me.

"You don't need to be here," she says. "I can coordinate your assignments with your teachers."

"Thank you. I just . . . I'd hate to miss another day. Especially photography lab."

Her eyes plead with me. "Don't . . ." She takes a shaky breath.

"What?" I ask in a whisper.

"Don't go to your locker."

My stomach churns like a concrete mixer as I push through the double doors that separate Admin from the school. The hall is like a freeway during rush hour—crowded with streams of people, all in a hurry. Everyone is wrapped up in their own conversations, but I feel gazes shift as they see me, hear the stutter of footsteps as I head to the locker bay.

"Yo, Grace Pierce!" someone calls.

I ignore it.

A girl I don't know says, "Why aren't you wearing orange, girl? That's going to be your new color."

"Oh my God," someone else cries. "Get a pic of us together."

I pull up short as a guy shoves against me and a phone is thrust in my face. I spin away, my heart thundering as I look for a way out. There are kids all around me, a loose circle growing tighter by the second. I search for someone I know and see a girl from English. "Brittney!"

She hesitates on the outside of the circle, and then I lose sight of her as someone pushes in front. *Harrison.*

"Hey, Grace," he says. "I've been wanting to talk to you. But you knew that, right? Guess you don't return calls anymore?"

"Harrison," I say. "It's . . . I'm sorry. I've been at the hospital."

Someone yells, "I heard your mom is faking it to avoid the FBI."

More voices chime in and I shake my head, horrified. "You can't fake a coma!"

"Why not?" Harrison snaps. "Apparently you can fake a fund."

"Hey, look at this," I hear from behind. There's a tug on my backpack. I turn to see a dark-haired girl with her hand around the Tiffany heart key chain I've had since grade school. "This is a cool key chain. Can I have this?"

"What?" I gasp. "Let go."

"Come on," she says. "Why not?" She yanks at the connecting ring. "You like taking things from other people. Why shouldn't we take things from you?"

She unhooks the chain and I grab her wrist. "Stop it!"

The others press in closer. I can't breathe, can't stop the rising panic. Then I spot movement at the edge of my vision—a flash of familiar white-blond hair. It's Cecily, pushing her way in.

She moves with authority, as if no one will challenge her—maybe because no one ever does. Loudly she says, "You guys. Seriously." She grabs the key chain out of the girl's hand and slaps it into my palm. Then she says, "Go home, Grace."

She spins away and I follow her through the crowd. "Thank you," I say, starting to shake now that I'm okay.

She freezes and turns back, her hands fisted. "Do not thank me," she hisses. "I'm already sorry I did that."

Before she can leave, I grab her arm. "Cecily, please. I need to talk to you. You have to let me explain."

"Explain what?" She shakes her arm free and then levels her glare at a few girls who have slowed to listen. They nudge each other and keep walking. She leans into my face. "That guy on the phone—he told you not to say anything. I heard him, Grace. Why would he say that unless you knew?"

"CC . . ." I flounder, words deserting me. "You have to believe me. You're my best friend."

Her eyes are shiny with tears, bright with anger. "I haven't told the FBI what I heard, but if the money doesn't turn up, I will."

My sob is swallowed by the sound of the first bell ringing. I watch her walk away as more sobs rack my body. My lungs strain for air and dark spots flicker in front of my eyes. *I have to get out of here.*

Instinct takes over and I lower my head and stumble toward the Admin doors. I pass the guidance center and then I'm back in the front office. When I go by Mrs. Joyce's desk, she stands up. "Grace!"

I don't stop.

"I'm sorry," she calls. "I'll have it repainted."

I don't stop until I get to my car, until I'm inside with the engine running and the doors locked.

Doesn't matter doesn't matter doesn't matter.

My hands are shaking, my vision blurry with tears, but I pull out of the parking space and hit the gas. I need to get home.

Mom will wake up. It'll be okay. Everyone will get their money back.

I drive by memory, by instinct, unaware of anything but my spinning thoughts. I don't even realize I've driven to the wrong house until I pull into the driveway and nearly collide with a white moving van. That wakes me up. I quickly reverse, and then . . .

My foot hits the brake.

Oh my God.

It *is* my house. Why is a moving van parked in my driveway?

Then I see the black sedan at the curb. And standing on my front porch is FBI Special Agent James Donovan.

18

August

"Where are we going?"

Sam. *Again.*

I sigh into the dark rumble of the bus, my forehead vibrating against the glass. It's giving me a headache, but it's also keeping me awake. There are too many dangers on this bus for me to sleep. Too many dangers in my head for me to dream.

I decide I might as well ask questions of my own. I turn my head so I can see Sam. The bus has one weak strip of light running down either side of the aisle, and sitting so close, I see that he's changed over the summer just as I have. His cheeks are sunken, and there are tiny lines of exhaustion by his eyes, as if time has marked him the way I marked lines through the calendar in Mom's room all through the month of June. "Why do you have a backpack?" I ask. "You couldn't have known I was leaving town."

"I like to be prepared."

"Really?" I fold my arms over my chest. "So what did you pack for a trip you didn't know you were taking?"

His eyes flicker up. "You show me yours and I'll show you mine."

"Sounds like fun, but I think I'll pass."

"Why? Hiding something?"

"All kinds of things." I smile. "Isn't that why you're following me?"

"What's in the pack, Grace?"

I feel the bulk of it safely wedged between the window and myself. "A camera. What's in yours?"

"A camera."

Our gazes lock. I want to hold on to my hate and mistrust, but I'm thrown by what I see in his eyes. He's telling the truth. The crazy thing is we both are. For a second, I'm choked with regret for everything lost. We shouldn't be here. *He* shouldn't be here.

Something buzzes and my thoughts scatter. He pulls a phone out of his back pocket. There's a text on the screen. With a glance, I steal some of the words.

Please—

—love you so—

The sender is MOM.

He puts the phone away and I turn to the window. I wish I hadn't looked. Outside, the night is an impenetrable black. I write on the window, my fingers spreading the ink of darkness across the dirty glass.

I'm sorry.

A zipper hums and then plastic rustles and tears. I smell something salty. Nutty.

"You hungry?"

Sam's voice. A low, almost embarrassed note I'm not used to hearing from him.

"I'm fine," I say to the window.

"Come on." His fingers appear in front of my face, part of a granola bar in his hand. The smell of peanut butter makes my stomach turn. Everything these days makes my stomach turn.

"You look like the old lady who sleeps behind the grocery store."

That gets my attention. "What?"

"You're too skinny." He offers me the bar again. "If you pass out from hunger, I'm going to have to carry you."

I don't want the bar, but the idea of him carrying me . . . I take a small bite. The granola sits like sand on my tongue but I force myself to swallow the rest of it. "Do you feed her, too? The lady behind the grocery store?"

I don't really expect him to answer, but when I glance his way, I catch an expression that makes my eyes widen. "You do, don't you?" He wads up the wrapper and I add one more mystery to the list that is Sam: the same guy who just punched out a man on the bus feeds homeless ladies.

"Where are we going, Grace?"

The monotonous hum of the engine fills my head, reverberating like his question, like every question I haven't been able to answer in the past three months. "I had a teacher in first grade," I tell him. "Miss Linda. She would stand at the classroom door every morning and hug us on the way in. She was skinny, and you could feel the bones of her hip against your face but you pressed against her anyway because she was everything good. One day we were coming back from music. I was third in line and Joey Saldo and Tiffany Everett were in front of me. The music teacher led the way into our classroom, and a second later I heard this weird cry and then her screams. The line stopped and I didn't know what was happening. Joey turned around and his face looked all wrong. 'What?' I asked, and he said, 'I think she's dead.' And I said, 'What?' and he said, 'Don't go in there.'"

Sam rubs at his arm. "Did you?"

"I did. I couldn't stop myself." I swallow. "That's what I'm doing now. I'm going to look at Miss Linda."

His face flickers from dark to light as a car's headlights pass us from the other direction. "What did you see?" he asks.

"Joey was right." I shudder. "I shouldn't have looked."

19

May

I call Uncle David before I'm even out of my car. They have a warrant to search the house and there's nothing I can do. "Cooperate," Uncle David tells me.

Donovan hands me a list of items they've been authorized to take:

> 30 ct tanzanite earrings
> Hermès Birkin bag
> Erte bronze statue
> Tarkay acrylic painting

It goes on for pages. Uncle David says there are lawyers working on the case. He says I don't need to talk to anyone if I don't want to.

I stand by the door while men with dollies go in. I watch them take what they say has been stolen until it feels as if they're boxing me up, too, a piece of me in every crate. They tear apart Mom's office with cool efficiency. I even help them open the safe. I watch it all until my rage grows large enough that I want to talk. I want to shout and scream. I want to know that someone hears me.

Donovan is upstairs. *In my bedroom.* He's studying the wall of photos. "You took all these?"

My nails bite into my palms. "You can't be in here. You have no right. This is my bedroom."

His blue eyes flicker with something that might be sympathy. "I'm sorry, Miss Pierce. It would be easier if you weren't here."

"Easier for whom?" I ask.

He turns toward my bookcase, his gaze stopping on the framed photos. Cecily and me at Disneyland in our mouse ears. Me hugging Tigger while he waves at the camera. "For both of us," he answers.

"Why are you doing this?" I follow up.

"Miss Pierce," he begins. He sighs. "You should have a lawyer present when we speak."

"I don't want a lawyer," I say. "I want answers."

He slides his hands into the pockets of his slacks. They're pressed, an even crease running down each leg. "We've been investigating the Family Fund for a long time."

"What do you mean, a long time?"

"We believe the first false statements were produced about six years ago."

The words spin through my head, buzzing like angry

wasps. "Six years? No. That isn't possible. That can't be right."

"We recovered evidence when we searched your mother's office. She reported investments and earnings when in fact there were none."

"That doesn't make sense," I say. "A person can't just make up a fund."

"It's known as a Ponzi scheme," Donovan explains. "A fund is created, such as the Family Fund, and at first the gains are excellent."

"They *are* excellent!"

"The fund manager touts a unique algorithm that allows them to earn more than other funds."

"My mom does have a unique algorithm." I press my lips together when I realize how it sounds—how it's making my mom sound.

"Early investors are rewarded handsomely and new investors are brought in. Statements continue to show excellent returns, but the money isn't invested at all, or only a portion of it is. Instead, the money is used to finance a lavish lifestyle on the part of the fund manager. In this case, your mother." He pulls a thick lump of folded papers from the inside of his coat pocket. He flips a few pages and begins to read. "A condominium in Newport Beach, California. Four automobiles, including a hundred-and-eighty-thousand-dollar Tesla. Trips to Santorini, Paris, and Budapest, and two weeks at a resort in Santa Lucia."

"That was a conference."

"Those trips were all taken in the past year." The paper crackles as he folds it up again. He studies me and I suddenly feel cold all over. "The problem with Ponzi schemes is they rely on a steady stream of new investors. You must have known about your mother's efforts to bring in new money. She used you to help her do it."

My hand reaches for the desk. Grabs hold. *What do they know? How much do they know?*

"Your face was on the marketing materials. It was more than that, though, wasn't it? You attended events with her; you spoke about the fund at mother-daughter clubs. You helped her tap into a market of two thousand families at your new school."

The whirring in my head grows. "That's not . . . You're making it sound bad."

"Because it looks bad. You left a very good private school to transfer to a public school in your junior year. Why would you do that?"

I press a hand to my forehead. "She wasn't cheating anyone. She wouldn't. A lot of the people who invested are my friends."

"What did you know, Miss Pierce? When did you know it?"

"My *best* friends!" I cry. Heat rises, painting my neck, my cheeks, my ears.

"Did your mother use you, Miss Pierce? Were you a victim as well? We just want to know what you know."

"You can't be here. You shouldn't be here!"

His voice is a whirring now, too. My head is filled with it.

"You have to face the situation. We have strong evidence."

"No." The tears I've been holding back spill over. "Evidence can be misleading."

"It can." He pulls a folded cloth from his back pocket and holds it out to me.

"I don't want that."

"It's just a handkerchief."

"I have tissues. Or are you taking those, too?"

He sighs. "I'm not the enemy, Grace." He holds out the handkerchief again. "May I call you Grace?"

"No," I snap, and I take the handkerchief. I wipe my eyes and my nose, then wad it into a ball. "Am I supposed to think of you as a friend?"

"No. But I could be an ally." He glances at my Disneyland pictures again. "I have a daughter, just a couple of years younger than you are."

"And that's why I should trust you, Special Agent Father?"

His expression softens. "She calls me that sometimes." He straightens the photo of Tigger. "But you don't need to trust me." He faces me again, his FBI mask firmly in place. "If the evidence is misleading and we're wrong, then there will be other evidence to prove her innocence. Wouldn't you agree?"

I swallow and nod.

"You could help us find it."

"Find what, exactly?"

"There are still things we don't know. Money trails that we need to follow. But they're well hidden. It might be that you know where they are."

"Money trails?"

"Paperwork. Notes. Transaction reports or receipts. You worked at her office over the past summer. Perhaps you saw something?"

"I sorted mail and reorganized the file cabinets."

"There might be a hidden safe, here in the house. Or an unusual hiding spot that only you would recognize."

"You're looking for ways to convict her."

"That's exactly what I'm looking for," he says, not shying away from my gaze. "But what if the information that's hidden could exonerate her?"

"*If* there's information."

"And if she's innocent," he adds.

"She is!" I insist.

"Then you'll help us?"

"No." I stiffen, my chin jutting forward. "I'll help my mother."

He nods, his eyes surprisingly kind. "For your sake, as well as the investors', I hope you can." He holds out one cupped palm. "And now, Miss Pierce, I'm going to need the keys to your car."

20

May

It's dark in my room. It may be dark outside; I don't know. I haven't moved from my bed in hours, and I don't want to turn on the light. Everything in here reminds me of Mom. The four-poster bed with the bright duvet cover she said felt like a painting by Henri Matisse. The bookcase of antique cameras. The words of photographer Steve McCurry that Mom had framed for me last Christmas: *If you wait, people will forget your camera and the soul will drift up into view.*

And of course, the wall of photos. Her face is in so many of them—the center of a million moments. The center of my life. There were times when I wished I had a dad. Father-daughter dances and art classes where we would work on macaroni picture frames for Father's Day. When Josephine's dad hoisted her on his shoulders for the Easter Day parade. But I thought it was fair because I had a mom like a movie star. She didn't drive a minivan and host bake sales. She wore silk skirts and high heels and she went to parties at night. She smoked long brown cigarettes and she drank champagne just because. One time, when Josephine dropped a bracelet in the toilet while she was pooping, her mom reached in for it. My mom would never have done that. My mom would have bought a new bracelet. She would have bought a new toilet.

I tilt my head to look back at the photos. I know them so well, even in the dark. Mom dancing at a little restaurant in Costa Rica. A photo of her from behind, her silhouette dark except for a thin line of smoke rising in the air. I never realized before, but most of the photos are just of her. I'm always the one taking the pictures. Now I wish there were more of us together.

"Did your mother use you?"

I shake my head at Agent Donovan's words. She wouldn't—she couldn't. He doesn't understand how it was—how it is. I pull myself up and stand, balancing on the bed as I study the collage. I press my fingers against a marketing photo Barry took when I was nine. It's one of my favorites. The backdrop is blue with soft white clouds, and there are reflectors everywhere. A hot yellow light pools around the stool where I sit upright. My shoulders are still imprinted with Barry's thumbs as he turned me just so.

Barry stood behind his camera to take the first test shot while Mom watched, her high heels making an impatient click on the floor. Barry snapped a few frames and then sighed. "Just look at that light."

My mother smiled at me as she smoothed cool fingers through my hair. "Don't be ridiculous, Barry," she said. "Grace *is* the light."

A well of pain unfurls in my chest, pressing hard against my lungs and my heart. Cracking me open. There's got to be evidence of her innocence. Something I can find. A link to the money. To the truth.

My hands push up through the pictures, pulling edges of photographic tape loose. I yank up one photo and then another. "Where is the evidence, Mom? Why won't you wake up and tell me where?" I rip a photo into strips of confetti and I shout, "Wake up!" There's no one to hear me, no one to stop me. No one.

I pull and tear and rip at every memory. I scream until I'm hoarse: "Wake up! Wake up and explain it to me. To everyone! Wake up wake up wake up!"

21

August

"Wake up!"

Someone is shaking me. I'm buried in confetti. I fling handfuls, armfuls. More confetti rains down. It's in my face. In my mouth. I can't—

"Wake up!"

I jolt into awareness. There's a shadow over me, a body. A sense of déjà vu rips through me. I kick up hard with a knee and hear a sharp, "*Shit!*"

I realize then that it's Sam.

He falls back into his seat as I struggle up in mine. The bus—I'm still on the bus and Sam is next to me. His body is hunched forward, his breath pained. "Shit," he says again.

I breathe hard into the dark, feeling the contours of the bus re-form around me. "What were you doing?" I hiss.

"Trying to wake you up. You were screaming."

"I was not," I say automatically. But the pieces of my

dream are still clinging like pieces of the photographs I tore up and then spent a sleepless night taping back together.

I shudder a breath and feel the sweat on my bare neck. "Let me out."

He shifts to the seat across the aisle, still doubled over. I grab my pack and move down the aisle, ducking to see through the windows. They might as well be covered in black paper. It's close to four a.m. and I wonder if we're still in Utah or if we've crossed into Colorado.

There's a scattering of people in the seats I pass, most of them asleep, including the guy who tried to sit behind me. The bathroom is a small closet at the very back. I use the toilet and run water over my face and through my hair. It feels good to rub my scalp and shake off the last shadows of sleep. I need to focus on what's ahead.

And Sam.

What do I do about Sam? I can't have him following me—I need to be alone. I pause, my gaze rising to my reflection in the cloudy mirror. I will be alone, though, won't I? As soon as Sam sees where I'm going, he won't hang around. He'll leave disappointed. He'll leave hating me.

But he'll leave.

My gaze shifts to my pack. It's a beautiful camera bag detailed in leather. It holds a new Leica camera and an adjustable lens. There's a side pocket with a flashlight, some snacks, and my water bottle. A small compartment is at the very bottom. I run my finger over the zipper. Beneath it is the soft bulge of a blue bandana that's been carefully folded around a pile of pills. Six blue Valium and seven white Xanax.

Enough to stop my heart.

I wonder if gray is the last color I'll see.

22

June

"Good morning, Lynn." I smile and press the back of my hand to my chin, where I can feel sweat beading. "It's a hot one today."

She looks up from her seat behind the nurses' station. "Morning." No smile in return. Again.

Hawthorn House is a long-term facility that promises Care for Life. After almost two weeks in the hospital, Mom had stabilized enough that they moved her here. That was three weeks and four days ago. Sometimes it's Margaret on duty and sometimes it's Terry, but usually it's Lynn. I liked her from the first time she came in to introduce herself. She looked just like Miranda from *Grey's Anatomy*. Short and sturdy. Familiar. She even had a blustery exterior like Miranda, but I could feel that she was hiding a soft heart.

"I brought cookies." Only half of the two dozen made it without breaking. It was kind of funny, really, balancing them on the two-mile bike ride to the bus's parking lot and then holding them over the air vent on the bus because the chocolate chips had melted in the sun. I imagine telling Lynn the story and I imagine her clucking her tongue and holding out her arms. *Come here and let me give you a hug.*

Sweat drips down my neck. It seems like I'm sweating more since I came inside to the air-conditioning. The heat must have affected my head. Why am I thinking about a hug? Miranda on *Grey's Anatomy* wouldn't hug someone just because they had to ride their bike. Miranda would say, *Don't invite me to your pity party, because I'm not coming.* Something like that.

"Chocolate chip," I say as I hand Lynn the plate.

The desk is a semicircle, large enough for three nurses to sit behind computers with a higher counter covered in maroon linoleum. Today there's a stack of flyers for the July Fourth celebration with boldfaced type: FORREST GUMP. RED, WHITE, AND BLUE CAKE. Lynn takes the plate and sets it on top of the counter.

"Thank you." Her voice is as flat as her brown eyes. I try not to take it personally. She's not here to be my friend. She's Mom's nurse. And she's great at her job. She lifts Mom, turns her, sits her up in the bed or in a chair. Monitors her vitals. Her food. Her catheter. She's a professional, and that's what she should be.

But I've heard her laughing with Dan and Elise, whose father is in room 5. I've seen her leaning over the counter and chatting with Saundra, whose mom is in room 2.

"Well," I say. "I hope you like them." With one more smile, I turn toward Mom's room. My computer bag bangs against my hip, and my skin feels overheated. It's just the sun, but it feels like a fever. It hurts to swallow. What if I'm sick? The thought is a relief. I could burrow under my comforter and have an excuse not to come out.

Mom is in bed. She looks like she's sleeping. Well, except for the NG tube taped over her nose that continues to feed her. But she's breathing on her own, and most of the machines are gone. In a while, Lynn and one of the other nurses will come in and move her to the chair. I leave the room for that part. It always feels as if they're arranging a doll, and when her head lolls or her arm flops awkwardly . . . I can't handle it. They call me back in when she's settled. I love that first second of seeing her in a chair as if she's . . . well, sitting up. Then I read to her or we watch TV. Today I might do her nails. I've touched up the gray in her hair. I even trimmed it a few days ago. It's almost pretty.

"Good morning," I say to Mom. Her room is bright with pale yellow walls. The window faces a corner of the parking lot where a lone tree is visible if you tilt your head just a little. I set my bag on the small square table beneath the TV and pull a pen from the outer pocket. The calendar by the door hangs from a nail and I hold it steady as I mark a line through another day. It's a calendar of cats, and June is a Siamese with gold-coin eyes. We've become adversaries, the cat and I. It stares at me and I stare back. "You don't know anything," I say. Its eyes seem to say *Yes, I do.* I remind myself it's a cat. Cats always look like they're disappointed in you.

"The art museum is doing a photography retrospective in September," I tell Mom. "I thought we could go."

I pull out my computer and set it on the table, which is already cluttered with magazines, coloring books, colored pencils, and a giant bag of Starbursts that's nearly empty. My mouth is always so dry. The candy helps.

The magazines are for Mom—I read articles about all the places we'll go when she's better. The coloring books are for me. It's like therapy without the cost of a thera-pist. Not that I know what a therapist costs, just that we couldn't afford one now. The administrator here informed me two days ago that Mom's insurance policy is under re-view. It's very likely we can't afford this place, either.

I told the administrator to talk to my uncle. Uncle David is handling the lawyers and the insurance and God knows what else. I just want to concentrate on Mom because I keep thinking if I focus hard enough I can will her back to life. Uncle David says I can't hide in this room forever. He says we need to talk. I've responded, very maturely, by avoiding him when he visits on Friday mornings and ignor-ing his phone calls. I keep putting him off with texts, but he's left four voice mails since yesterday, and I know I can't put him off much longer.

"So," I say loudly, more to distract myself than because I think Mom will suddenly open her eyes. Still. I check to be sure she doesn't. "I found an anthill out back yesterday.

I took pictures, and I swear it looked like they were making punctuation marks. A question mark, a semicolon. Apparently, we have grammatically correct ants."

"Grace?"

I look toward the door. Lynn is standing there, expressionless. "You should turn on the TV."

She doesn't wait for me to respond. She comes in the room and takes the remote from the table. The TV flashes on with a loud ping, the screen switching to the local cable network.

"It's been five weeks since Janelle Pierce was served notice of the investigation and five weeks since she suffered a stroke," the reporter is saying. "Authorities say they'll wait until she regains consciousness to arraign her on all charges."

"Charges?" I repeat.

Then the scroll of words begins.

JANELLE PIERCE INDICTED
ON THIRTY-SIX COUNTS OF WIRE FRAUD.

"Federal investigators are still trying to account for all the money invested. Unsubstantiated reports suggest there is more than forty-five million dollars still unaccounted for."

Numb, I turn toward Lynn. She's staring at me.

I think about the plate of cookies I baked and carried here so carefully. I know that right now, they're in a trash can.

"She didn't do anything wrong," I say. "They accused

her, and now they have to look like they're right. They're doing this because she's in a coma and because she can't defend herself."

She blinks slowly, deliberately. As if she's saying *Thirty. Six. Counts.*

Panic fills me, bringing me to my feet. "She's innocent, and I'm going to prove it. You can tell everyone that I won't stop until I do." I gather myself, pride the only thing keeping me on my feet. "I'd like to be alone with my mother, if you don't mind."

"Whatever you like." She drops the remote on the bed and walks out.

Not Miranda at all.

Indicted on thirty-six counts.

A shiver rolls over my clammy skin. Doubt claws at my belly, and suddenly I'm running for the restroom. I barely make it there before I'm sick. My stomach heaves, doubling me over as everything comes up.

No. It can't be true. That would mean . . . No! My stomach convulses again. *I believe in her. The only choice I have is to believe.*

When I'm strong enough to stand, I flush the toilet and stumble to the sink. I rinse out my mouth and splash water over my face. When I've got my breath under control again, I return to Mom's room. Her eyes are closed. It's always been her eyes that could make you laugh. Could make you believe. Could make you trust.

It's up to me now. I have to be her eyes. Her voice.

"Where, Mom?" I watch the soft, steady rise and fall of her chest. She's in there. She's listening—I know she is. I stand by the bed and reach for her cold hand. I rub the freckle on her finger. My eyes fill when I realize what I'm doing. I'm nearly eighteen and I'm still looking for secrets under a freckle.

It's not as if I haven't been searching since Donovan left. But where do you begin? How do you look for something you might not recognize even when you see it? I lean closer, ignoring the smell of sickness that clings to us both.

"Where's the proof, Mom? Where's the money?"

23

August

The darkness is slowly becoming a deep gray. It's been fourteen hours since I left Phoenix, and my aching body wants nothing more than to get off this bus. But my stomach disagrees, rolling with a sense of dread as each minute ticks by and we get closer. The colors of daybreak are out there, just waiting for light to bring them to life. How many mornings did I wait for the sunrise, reading hope into the burst of color as if it were personally delivered by God? Now the light doesn't even have the power to warm. It seems indifferent. Like God.

My head is throbbing, a hangover from the nightmare. "Do you have them, too?" I ask Sam, turning suddenly.

I catch him watching me, but I have no idea what he's thinking. Guys used to watch me, and I could read the appreciation in their smiles. I had pretty hair and a pretty face. Curves in all the right places. Now nobody looks at me and likes what they see.

"Do I have what?" Sam asks.

"Nightmares."

His expression turns wary.

"I used to believe in all the clichés," I explain. "'Time heals all wounds.' That sort of thing. But is that really what happens? If I live long enough, will I stop caring? Even in my sleep?" A bleak sigh escapes. "Can you stop caring even in your sleep?"

Something flickers in the depths of his gold eyes. "If you're tired enough."

I think of all the times I've seen him out running. Head down, arms and feet flying, as if he were being chased. Or maybe he's just trying to outrun himself. If I could, I'd do the same thing. His thumb rubs at his arm, and I want to put my hand over his and make him stop. Instead, I turn back to the window.

The minutes pass in silence, the rumble of road and engine lulling me toward something numb and almost peaceful. Shadows slowly become rising hills and thick-trunked trees with wide, leafy arms. The ground becomes a wet brown and the highway a cracked and oily gray. The desert is gone and the mountains are moving nearer. The San Juan Mountains are somewhere to the east, visible even now.

It won't be there. I won't find it.

But I might.

I shift, rearranging my pack, which has been doubling as my pillow. A trail of color outside catches my eye, and I realize there are wildflowers growing alongside the highway.

I spread my fingers on the glass, squinting to see better. "I would have noticed those first," I murmur.

Sam shifts beside me. "What?"

I tap on the window. "If I were going to photograph this, I would have started with the flowers. I would have filled the frame with them and never even noticed the cracks in the asphalt. You," I say, "would have photographed the cracks."

His shoulder brushes mine as he leans closer. "Probably."

I try to ignore his nearness and focus on the fissures in the road, the way they widen and then narrow. "How do you ever see the flowers again once you've seen the cracks?"

His breath is warm on my neck. "Were you going to hand it in?"

My pulse jumps. "What?" I turn, and he shifts back.

"The money. If I weren't here, would you turn in the forty-five million?"

Acid bubbles in my gut, burns up my windpipe. "You're so sure that the money exists?"

His eyes narrow. "Yes."

"How nice that must be for you—that certainty."

"People like your mother always find a way to protect their own."

"People like my mother?" It's strange, this feeling of pain. You hold on to it long enough, it makes you want to share it. It makes you want everyone to feel as bad as you do. Anger lifts my chin. "You don't know the first thing about my mother."

"I don't believe, not for a minute, that she left you with nothing."

"No," I say. "What you can't believe, what you really can't face, is that you got greedy and you got duped. You and your mom, like every other investor, believed in the unbelievable eighteen percent you were promised. You didn't question that, did you? No, that all sounded just great to you." My mouth is running off without me, and I can't for the life of me stop. "What about betrayal, Sam? Can you believe in that? Can you believe in impossible, un-fucking-believable betrayal? Because that's the real question."

I'm panting, my breath coming hard, but his is, too, his chest rising and falling and his eyes—his eyes are wet and staring.

Static bursts from the speaker system, followed by the driver's voice. "Twenty minutes to Ridgway, folks. Be sure to double-check for your belongings before exiting the bus."

Sam gathers his pack and I gather mine. I think, mostly, we're gathering ourselves. I force my heart back into slow, steady beats. Every time I give in to my emotions, it takes a toll. I feel like a washrag, wrung out and frayed at the edges.

Again the speaker system buzzes to life. "Weather is fifty-four degrees right now with an expected high of seventy-five and some rumblings of a summer storm later in the day. I hope you had a comfortable trip, and I hope you'll travel with Rhodeways again."

The speaker clicks off. People begin shifting in their seats, standing to pull bags from the rack above.

Sam waits in the aisle. His feet are planted wide, like he owns the ground he stands on, but his hand is gripping the seat, as if he's afraid to let go. There's anger in his gaze—but there's also an unmistakable fear. "I believe in that money," he says. "I believe in forty-five million dollars."

The air brakes hiss as the bus slows on the outskirts of town.

"I thought you were smarter than that," I say. "I thought you knew better than to believe in anything at all."

24

June

I tried to tell Uncle David no. I did tell him no—three times—but he kept saying it would be good for me—good for us. Then he just said, "Please. We need to talk." News of the indictment broke five days ago. He tried to warn me it was coming, but I ignored his calls. Now I'm afraid of what else he needs to tell me.

So here we are at a driving range I've never been to, and at least that's a blessing. There are five other men hitting balls, and I don't know any of them. They don't know me.

Today was one of those decent days in June—hot, but with enough of a breeze that you hoped it meant the summer would be a mild one. Now, at seven o'clock, there's still another hour of daylight, and it's so cool it actually feels good being outside.

I feel good being outside.

My golf glove is a crumpled wad after being stuffed in my bag all this time. It's wonderful to stretch my fingers into the leather, to watch it take shape again. I feel like I'm stretching back into my old life, with my golf shorts and polo, hair in a pony and red visor settled low on my forehead.

A door closes, and I look toward the pro shop. Uncle David is walking toward me with a large mesh bucket of balls.

"It's been a while since I've done this," he says. He tips the bucket on the tray by my spot. The balls pour out, clacking against each other, a few bouncing wild. I gather them back in the pile with the head of my golf club. Uncle David empties the other half of the balls at his station next to mine. He straightens, smiling. "Remember the first time I brought you to the driving range?"

"A little," I say. I was only six, but the truth is I do remember. Mom had to work and my nanny was out of town, so I ended up with Uncle David for the day. He brought me to a driving range and presented me with a bright orange plastic golf club and Wiffle balls to match. I liked setting my balls up on tees and then trying to make them fly. I copied Uncle David's movements and rituals. Swinging a golf club seemed like a kind of dance to me and I would hold my finish like a ballerina at the end of a solo.

"You still have a great finish," Uncle David says, as if he's sharing the same memory. I suppose he is. He reaches in his bag for his own glove. "Go ahead. Let's see what you've got."

I line up a ball and take a few practice swings to loosen my back and shoulders. I'm holding an eight-iron, and the grip feels like a second skin. I've missed this. I settle in my stance and then let it launch. The golf ball makes a satisfying *crack* as it connects with the face of the club. I follow the flight of the ball, squinting as it arcs into the setting sun. It hits the ragged grass of the driving range and rolls to a spot nowhere near where I was aiming.

"A little rusty," I say, reaching with my club for another ball.

"You'll find the groove," he says. He takes out a club and turns his back to me.

For a while, we're both quiet. I breathe in the smell of grass and dirt with a smile. The world narrows to the crack of balls hitting metal and the rhythm of my swing. I haven't played golf since Mom's stroke. It feels good, though. Hitting range balls has always been a way for me to escape. Focusing on a tiny white ball has a way of clearing your mind.

But some things you can't escape for long. I'm halfway through my pile of balls when Uncle David stops to watch me hit a five wood.

He leans his hand on the butt of his club and nods in approval. "Looks good. Nice loft on that club."

"Thanks. It feels good." I roll another ball into place.

"Aunt Caroline and I are hoping you'll join the golf

team at Cactus High School next year. We've already spoken to the coach."

My head shoots up. "What? You've spoken to the coach? Why?"

"It's June, Grace. School starts in two months. It's time to make plans."

My fingers clench around the grip of my club. "I'm not going to Cactus High."

"It's a great school, and it's close to our house."

"I'm staying in *my* house."

He sighs, wiping his forehead with the back of his arm. A line of golf carts motors past—a last group coming off the course. The noise eats away what's left of my calm.

Is this what he wanted to talk about?

I should have stuck to *no*. He's my only real family, but that doesn't mean he has the right to take over my life. We're not even that close. When I was little, he took me places sometimes and bought me the kind of lollipops that had candy inside. Is that enough for me to love him? Or should I love him because he's Mom's brother? He looks like her—but only if you add a photo filter that dulls some of the color. He's eight years younger, same wiry frame, same coloring, same blue-gray eyes, but without any of Mom's vibrancy. Even the two of them aren't close.

Uncle David lived in Chicago until four years ago, when he and Aunt Caroline moved back to Phoenix. They decided to pick a neighborhood thirty minutes away from

130

us. We get together for holidays and birthdays, but for the past three years, the focus has always been on the twins, because, well, they're twins and they're adorable. There's not a lot of family bonding. I've never seen Mom fight with Uncle David, but they don't hug either. And one time, years ago, I remember Mom saying that Uncle David had been spoiled, and like all spoiled things, he'd grown up soft. I don't think I was supposed to hear her, but I never forgot. And maybe I've always had that in the back of my mind. Another filter to frame the way I see him.

"We need to make plans," he says. He suddenly looks tired. "You need to get registered, pick your classes, make sure you're on schedule for graduation. Cactus has a great photography program—"

I bend down over another ball. "I haven't decided what I'm going to do in the fall."

"You're going to finish high school, of course."

My backswing is fast, my swing plane too steep, and when I come through the ball, I hit the ground first. Hard earth and yellowing grass spray up, and tremors of pain vibrate through my arm at the impact. Tears spring to my eyes.

"You okay?" he asks.

"I'm fine," I snap. I reach for another ball.

"Grace." His club drops over mine, stopping me. My heart is pounding, and I want to scream at him to go away. "Look, I know you'd rather not think about all this, but you have a future. Aunt Caroline and I both feel it will help if you focus on that right now. We can help you map out a plan for college. Look at your grades and test scores and see what scholarships are available. There's also community college for the first two years to keep expenses down."

I shake my club out from under his. He sighs, but he steps back as I line up another ball. "You'll have to work," he continues, "but not right away. We thought you could play golf for your new school. That's why we spoke to the coach. It will give you the opportunity to make new friends. To rebuild your life."

"No." I shift into my stance, but I hardly see the ball through my wet lashes. "You live too far from the rehab facility, and I don't have a car."

"You can borrow Aunt Caroline's car sometimes. And you won't be going every day."

"Yes. I will." I miss the ball again, slicing it weakly this time so it bounces aimlessly through the grass. I'm going from bad to worse. I move back to my bag and shove the club in. "I've had enough," I say.

His expression is full of pity. "Your home is with us now, Grace."

I stiffen. "Thank you, but I already have a home."

He puts away his club, too. The sun is sinking, and it's just the two of us out here now. "Grace, you need to listen—"

"No." I shake my head. "I'll take classes online if I need to, but I'm not leaving my house."

"I'm sorry, but you have to."

"I don't. I'm nearly eighteen, and—"

"Grace." Something about his voice stops me.

His eyes meet mine. So much like hers . . . but not. "The government is taking possession of the house. They're going to sell it at auction, and the proceeds will be used to reimburse investors."

I cover my mouth, stifling a cry. "They can't."

"I'm afraid they can. You've got until August tenth to vacate."

"No." I shake my head furiously. "I'm not leaving."

"You don't have a choice."

"Then the FBI will have to come on August tenth," I say. "They'll have to take the keys out of my hands."

"It won't be the FBI," he says flatly. "It will be the Marshals Service, and they'll take the keys and physically remove you from the house if necessary."

A chill runs up my spine.

He rubs his face again. "Please, Grace. You're only making this harder on yourself."

"I'm the one making it harder?" I rip off my golf glove and wad it back into a ball.

"You've got to quit hanging on to—"

"What?" I demand. "To my mother? She's not dead, or have you forgotten that?"

"I'm not the enemy," he says. "Aunt Caroline and I pray every day that she gets better. But when she does wake up, she's going to prison. You need to face who she is."

"I know who she is. You're the one who's convicting her without knowing what she's done or why she's done it. Why can't you wait for her to wake up?"

"I understand how much you want to believe her. Even if she weren't your mom, Janelle has always had a way about her. Your mother is the light that draws the moth, Grace. But the moth can beat its wings and the light doesn't care. The moth can throw itself into the heat and die and the light doesn't care. The light only cares about shining."

Tears burn at the back of my throat. "Just leave me alone, okay? Leave us both alone." I grab my bag of clubs and swing the strap over my back. I'll take a bus home. Hell, I'll walk the eight miles if I have to.

Uncle David is wrong. My mom did love me. *She does.* She wasn't a helicopter mom—she never had time for that. But she only ever wanted the best for me.

"I'm not too busy for you, Grace. I'm busy because of you."

She wanted me to have a life without all the struggles she faced. That's why she started the Family Fund in the first place. If something happened with her business, then it's because she was trying to provide for me.

"Grace, wait." I hear Uncle David behind me, his clubs rattling with every step. "Let me drive you home."

Home.

For how much longer?

I swallow my pride because I have no idea where a bus

stop is near here, and I'm not sure I can walk home carrying clubs with my knees ready to buckle. I need to find that evidence. I don't tell Uncle David, but that's why I can't move.

Somewhere in that house, there's a link to the money.

I've been through the closets, through old coat pockets and hatboxes. I've searched behind photos, pulling the backing away to see if there are slips of paper hidden inside. I've lifted sofa cushions and shined a flashlight under every piece of furniture in case it was taped there. This weekend, I went into the attic in the garage. I pulled everything out of every box, while my skin crawled with the stickiness of cobwebs and something rustled from the roof above. I tried to keep my flashlight from illuminating the scattered pellets of rat poop. Tried not to think of the rats that might be there . . . somewhere. When I found a crawl space behind a box, it took everything I had to follow the narrow passage and not vomit.

And still nothing.

My mind spins on the silent drive home. Where else do I look? Where would Mom hide something small? Something important? Did she tell me and I just didn't recognize the hint at the time?

I've gone over every conversation we had in the past couple of months. When we talked about a new kind of granola, were we really talking about granola? I emptied out the box two days ago, my heart pounding like an idiot's. It's like putting together a jigsaw puzzle without

having the box to show you what it's going to look like
when you're done.

A puzzle!

Oh my God.

I nearly cry out with relief.

That's it.

25

August

Ridgway, Colorado, is a small town surrounded by sloping green hills and farmhouses framed by mountain peaks. We've driven into a painting.

I step off the bus, glad for the solid ground under my boots and the fresh breeze that cools my face and neck. I feel almost feverish, but that's due to my unwelcome shadow. Sam's footsteps grind through the gravel just behind me as I head for the convenience store. His noisy steps follow me down the aisles, where I buy a Diet Coke and Sam gets two donuts and a coffee. The tension is so thick I have to swallow before I can ask the clerk about hiring a taxi.

"We don't have taxis."

"But . . ." I blink in confusion. "How do people get around?"

"Hitchhike," he says. He's a guy in his twenties with

bleached blond hair and a vest covered in *Doctor Who* buttons. "That's what I do."

"Don't be an ass," Sam says, planting one hand on the counter. "She's not going to hitchhike."

I bristle. I don't need him protecting me. Protecting his investment. "Thanks," I say to the clerk.

Sam follows me into the parking lot and then to the corner of the main road. The town stretches before me, a wide street of quaint buildings lined with trees. Beyond I see the range of mountains where I'm headed. They're no more than an outline against the horizon, as if someone is drawing a picture and hasn't had time to sketch in all the details.

When I put up my thumb, Sam steps in front of me, his voice a growl. "Stop it, Grace."

"You're blocking the view."

"You know you're not hitchhiking."

"Really?" I blink up at him. "You know that, too?"

"Call a limo service or whatever it is rich people do."

"Limos are so dated," I say with a dismissive flip of one hand. "I always prefer a Lamborghini, though they've really got to do something about their cup holders."

"Is that supposed to be funny?"

"You tell me," I say. "You seem to know everything." I wish these stupid boots had five-inch heels so I could look him in the eye. "Let me ask you something, Sam. Did you know everything about your brother?"

He stills, his breath drawing in with a hiss.

"Did you know he played with death?" I feel around with each question, searching for a soft spot. For a bruise I can press with my words. "There were stories about you, too. People said you played along with him. Were you a part of the games that killed him?"

His eyes fill with shards of amber hate.

Good. Hate is so much easier. Hate is so much safer.

I turn my back to him and start walking. There's a man with a small white dog, and I wonder what he sees when he nods my way. I used to be the face of the Family Fund. I used to be the face of hope and a bright future. And now what? Does he see my ugliness? Does he know what lives inside of me? This is what I've become. *Who* I've become.

My mother's daughter.

26

August

We've covered two miles in about forty minutes. I've had my thumb in the air for most of it, and Sam hasn't tried to stop me again. I think he's decided I'm bluffing and he's going to wait it out. Either that, or he hopes I'll get picked up and chopped into tiny little pieces.

My legs are already tired, which is not good. We've been on a gradual climb through town, and I'm starting to think I should have planned this out better.

Or planned this out at all.

No taxis?

How did Mom travel in those days? I don't think I ever asked if she drove here or took a plane and rented a car. I must have imagined her floating to Ridgway on her gossamer angel wings. And now that I'm on the side of this dusty road, I can't picture her here at all.

Did she laugh at my stupidity? Was it a game to her? If

she could see me now, on this pathetic quest, she'd probably laugh herself into another coma. Acid burns in my stomach. I need to get this over with.

I stop to take a breath and check my watch. There are about five miles to the turnoff, and another nine miles of dirt road after that. And then the hard part starts. At this rate, I won't make it by dark.

I thrust my thumb back into the air. Am I not doing it right? Is there some trick? How can I know the derivative of a polynomial but not how to get a ride? I'm so useless.

I hold my thumb higher and let the breeze cool my raised face. The air is thinner at this elevation, but after so much time in the care facility, I'd forgotten how clean air can go right to your bloodstream and make you feel awake. Best of all, there's no sickness. No latex gloves and daily updates of bodily functions. If only I could forget why I'm here and where I'm going. If only I could forget who I was and become some nameless seventeen-year-old with nice eyes and a bad haircut. I'd climb on the back of a cute boy's bike and we'd ride off together like in a book.

Snakes shed their skin. Why can't I?

Because, a voice in my head says, *even when they shed their skin, they're still snakes.*

A car zooms by. Dust flies into my upturned eyes and coats my throat. I cough until my eyes water, and when I wipe my cheeks, I feel the grit of sand on my skin. On the horizon, the mountains are no closer. Another car speeds past, and by the time I stick up my thumb, it's gone. I glare at Sam, my feet skimming dirt as I walk backward.

"No one will pick me up with you here."

He barely gives me an annoyed glance.

"I'm serious," I snap. "You look frightening. Big and . . . lumbery."

"Lumbery?"

"At least take off the hood."

He's put the sweatshirt back on and pulled up the hood. "It's cold."

I gasp with pretend shock. "You can feel the cold? I thought you only projected it."

I stick my thumb out again, squinting against the sun as I turn for a white Prius covered in peace stickers. I curse as it goes by. Even environmental hippies are passing me. I check my watch, though time hasn't miraculously slowed. It's 10:40 now. Friday. Sometimes, Mom would go into the office late on Fridays. She'd drink her coffee, read on her iPad. I tried to log in to it after she had the stroke, but I didn't know the password. Like an idiot, I tried every possible version of *Grace*.

Enough. No more thinking. No more walking.

My fingers fumble with the zipper of my jacket. Finally, it's off and belted around my waist. My T-shirt isn't what you'd call sexy, but underneath I've got on a black racerback bra that I wear for golf. It's not Victoria's Secret, but it shows plenty of skin. I reach for the hem of my shirt and tug it up. Before I get it over my head, I hear a muttered curse and the shirt is being yanked down.

"What are you doing?" Sam demands.

"Getting a ride."

"Not like that, you're not."

"Watch me."

He points to my jacket. "Put it back on."

"I didn't ask for your opinion," I say, holding my ground. "And in case you've forgotten, you're an uninvited guest."

His face is flushed, his eyes blazing. "Put on the damn jacket, Grace."

"Not until I get a damn ride!"

He reaches for the jacket and I swat his hand away. But he's got his grip on a sleeve and tugs me toward him. I fall into his chest, punching him with the sides of my fists until he's forced to hold my arms.

"Stop it!" he shouts.

"Let go of me!" I shout back.

"I'm not going to watch you get raped!"

"Why not?" I cry. "Most people want to see me *dead*." I shove him again, and his arms drop. I step back, panting.

He stares at me, his mouth open with obvious shock.

My eyes sting, but I refuse to cry. "I get a few death threats every week. They come in the mail, along with bills that can't be paid. I keep a file, though the FBI assures me they aren't credible." I hug myself with shaking arms. "I'm not sure what makes a threat credible. Maybe if there are no typos or if—"

"Grace." His voice cuts me off. "Shit." He pushes off the hood and runs a hand through his hair. "Are you really trying to hitchhike?"

"What did you think I was doing?"

"Trying to piss me off?"

"That was just a bonus." I straighten my jacket and take another shuddering breath. "The place I'm going is about thirteen miles from here, and I don't have any other way to get there."

"No Lamborghinis in Ridgway?" But there's a wry tilt to his lips that softens his words.

"Nope. And I forgot my magic wand."

With a sigh, he tugs at the loose jacket around my waist and pulls it free. He holds it out. "Put that back on."

I stare at it, uncertain. "I still need to get a ride."

"I'll get you a ride."

"How?"

He looks at the highway and then points to a clump of trees about a hundred yards up. "I'll hide back there. As soon as someone stops, I'll come out."

I slide the jacket on and for the first time I wonder about how awful I must look. "What if no one stops?"

His gaze slides down my body and then back up. His voice deepens. "They'll stop."

A flush pulses under my skin as if his hands touched me everywhere his gaze just did. I look away and tug the zipper to my neck.

"Just hold up your thumb. I'll be over there being . . . lumbery."

My eyes flash to his, but he's already striding toward the trees.

I wait until he's half hidden and then stick out my thumb. The fourth vehicle to pass slows down and then pulls off to the dirt shoulder. It's a white Ford truck, and I shield my eyes as it jerks to a stop just ahead of me. The side reads JOY FARMS and there are slatted crates stacked in the truck bed. The dust hasn't even settled when Sam is by my side. The window rolls down, and I see an older man with gray hair in a pony and a tattoo on his shoulder that reads JUST PEACHY.

"I didn't see there was two of you," he says.

"Nature was calling," Sam replies, leaning in with a friendly smile.

"Where you headed?" he asks.

Sam shifts his gaze to me.

I take my turn at the open window, breathing in fruit and coffee. "County Road 7. I'm wondering . . . hoping . . . I can pay you to take me off the beaten path a little ways."

"How little?"

"Trailhead about nine miles in."

"Blue Lakes, huh?" He scratches at the stubble beneath his chin. "Hop in and I'll get you there. Name is Joe, by the way." He pats the seat with a grin, but before I can climb in, Sam has his hand on my arm. "I'll take the middle. I know you get carsick if you don't have the window."

He slides in and I catch Joe giving him a knowing wink. He thinks we're together. He thinks Sam is jealous. And a traitorous part of me wishes he was right. That it wasn't hate and betrayal between us. That we could rewind to those few minutes when he was joking with me. When he looked at me as if he didn't hate me at all.

I slide in beside him, awkward with my own thoughts. I don't want to touch him, but I can't help it—there's barely room in the cab for the three of us. So I turn away, pretending an interest in the view. He's protecting his money, not me. But it still feels nice, and nice things make me unravel.

Joe puts the car in drive. "You ever been to Blue Lakes before?"

I shake my head.

"Well," he says, "you're in for a treat."

27

July

I can do this carefully.

Or I can do this with a hammer.

I study the nine puzzle boxes that line the top of a heavy wood credenza in the game room. The puzzle boxes were gifts from Mom. I'd find one in my Christmas stocking each year. I loved puzzles but these were tricky. I'd drink my hot chocolate while I worked through the series of springs and levers that would open them. Most years I ended up frustrated trying to get to what was inside.

"It's about the sense of achievement, Grace. That's the treasure," Mom said.

"I'd rather have an actual treasure," I replied.

Mom laughed. "That's my girl."

Now the boxes stare back at me and I wonder if there's a real treasure here after all.

Maybe the proof has been here this whole time.

The first box is shaped like a star. I push on one point and a bit of wood slides open from the bottom. I work at each panel until the star opens like a flower.

Empty.

The second box is also empty.

The third refuses to cooperate. That happens sometimes. The heat makes the wood swell and the pieces won't slide no matter what you do. I pick up the hammer and set the box on the carpet. With both hands on the thick handle, I strike the octagon dead center. The wood splinters like kindling. I sift through the pieces. Nothing.

I smash the next box, and the next box and the next.

I read once about behavioral therapy where the patient is encouraged to physically beat on old cars with a steel bat. It made no sense to me. If your life is falling apart, why do you want to destroy anything else?

Now I understand.

I shove back my sweaty hair. My face is wet again with tears. I'm so sick of my useless tears. Around me the carpet is strewn with broken bits of boxes. I grip the hammer. Striking at the boxes makes me want to strike out, period. It makes me want to put this hammer through a wall. Through every wall.

"Where, Mom? Where did you hide the evidence? And what did you do with the money?"

28

August

Joe drops us at the end of a long and bumpy dirt road. He won't take any money and he hands Sam and me a peach from a crate in the back of his truck. "Have a good hike," he calls as he wheels the truck around and drives off.

It's nearly noon and the sun is just over my left shoulder, the sky blue above the makeshift parking lot. Sam's sweatshirt is already off and stuffed into his pack, but my jacket feels like another layer of protection. Against what, I'm not sure. The truth?

There are four trucks and a couple of jeeps parked in the dirt. In the center of the lot, there's a bathroom surrounded by flies and a water spigot that's splashing like a miniature waterfall into a bowl. A woman with a wide-brimmed hat is crouched beside it, giving water to a dog that's slurping more out of the dish than into its mouth. A fringe of trees marks the perimeter and I circle slowly, taking it all in.

The air is so fresh I could close my eyes and imagine myself in a produce section of a grocery store. In fact, that's exactly what I do. With my eyes shut, I take a bite of my peach. I nearly groan at how good it is. Juice fills my mouth and drips down my chin. I take more bites, savoring the sweetness. It's maybe the best peach I've ever had. It makes me hope that this place is magical after all. That I'm going to climb up to the lake and find that fairy tales are sometimes true.

"This is it?" Sam asks. "This is going to lead to my money?"

I sigh as reality settles back onto my shoulders. Maybe a lake is just a lake. Maybe a peach is just a peach. I throw the pit into a wide metal trash bin. "Not exactly." The trail is to my right, marked by a large wooden sign. Behind panes of glass, there's a map of the trail system and flyers with headlines like *Wilderness Wise* and *Use Restrictions*.

Eyeing me, obviously unconvinced, he strides the few paces to study the map. "You're going to climb three point three miles up a mountain? Why?"

"Because this was my mother's favorite place." My mind fills with a photo of Mom standing by the lake. So young and so pretty. Her smile as wide as the spectrum of light. And I think again that there has to be an explanation. Even now, after the things I've discovered, I want to believe in that smile. "My mom loved this place." I wipe at the sticky juice on my chin. "She would hike up here every few years and come home reborn. That's what she said. She said that when you get to the top, you're half a step from heaven."

He walks back to me, his head shaking with every step. "You don't do the things you've done because you're in the mood for a pretty hike."

"She's dying, Sam." I blurt the words. I don't know how to say them any other way.

"What do you mean?"

I shift my feet, bracing myself against another surge of memory. I want to shut off my emotions like the water spigot but the ugliness is leaking through my veins and through my voice. "She had a second stroke two days ago," I say. "Her heart is still beating but her brain is dead. She's being kept alive by machines but the doctors want to pull the plug."

His face has gone pale.

"It's up to my uncle, and he's left it up to me. I told the doctor to pull the plug. That's how I said it, too. Nothing polite and refined, the way my mother would want. See, I was always aware that I could be talking to a potential investor. If they liked me, then they might want to give my mom their money. And everyone always liked me. Except, possibly, for you. But you don't like anyone. Anyway," I say, my words jerky and uneven, "my uncle was shocked when I said that. He insisted the hospital give me a few days to be sure. To really think it through. So she's lying in a hospital bed, being kept alive in case her organs can be harvested. As it turns out, my mother's death could be good news for some people. She wasn't registered as an organ donor, but my uncle and I get to make that decision, too. Doctors can take her liver and her heart and her kidneys. Her organs can go to people so desperate, they won't even care that they came from Janelle Pierce."

"Grace—"

"Wait a minute," I say, cutting him off with an exaggerated slap to my forehead. "Maybe we can sell them on the black market. You can have some of the pancreas money. Do they transplant pancreas?" I frown. "I'm not sure. Kidneys, definitely. Probably not her lungs. She was a smoker," I add. "It's why she had high blood pressure. Why she probably had the first stroke."

"Grace, you need to sit—" He reaches for my arm, but I step away.

"So on Sunday at one, I'm expected back at the hospital so I can hold her hand when they take her off life support. My. Mom." Despite myself, despite everything, my eyes fill with hot tears. "She'll be gone. Terminated. And I don't even know who she is anymore. So I thought, I'll go to the place she said she loved. The place that meant so much to her. Maybe I'll even find her up on the mountain. And before she dies, I'll see if Blue Lakes was everything she promised." My mouth lifts in a parody of a smile. "My mom, as you know, was famous for her promises."

His throat works, but if there are words, none make it out.

I don't want words. I just want him to go before I fall apart completely. I pull the money from my front pocket and count it out. I have one hundred and eighty-three dollars left. "Here," I say. "Take it. I'm sorry it's not thirty-five thousand, but it'll get you back to Phoenix."

He still doesn't move, doesn't reach for the money. "On the bus, when you fell asleep. When you were dreaming? You said something."

My breath catches.

"You said it's there. You kept muttering it over and over."

"It was just a dream. It doesn't mean anything." I look him straight in the eye. "It doesn't mean what you think it means."

His left hand scratches his upper arm. His nail beds turn white with pressure and I wince. It must hurt. It has to. It's like he doesn't even know he's doing it.

"If you don't mind, I think I'll see for myself."

"And if I do mind?"

He shrugs and shifts his pack higher. "I'm following you anyway."

I shove the money in my pocket. "I just want to do this alone."

He looks toward the mountain. His expression is as bleak as the jagged peaks that rise dark against the sky. "We're always alone, Grace."

29

July

The original owners of our house, the ones who built it, created the perfect hiding spot.

It was in the master bedroom, set in the back wall, and looked exactly like an air-conditioning vent. I'd never noticed it before—Mom had angled a love seat in front of it, along with an ottoman and a small table that was always piled with books.

Then three years ago, Mom remodeled the whole master suite. During the demo, the contractor was checking the air ducts and he pulled off the door and the filter and discovered a sealed space the size of a microwave.

Mom wasn't home, so he showed me what he'd found.

"Mom," I said when I got her on the phone. "Guess what the contractor found in your room behind the air-conditioning vent?"

"Ahh," she said. "I forgot to tell him about that."

"So you knew!"

"Ingenious, isn't it?"

"Why didn't you ever tell me?"

"I don't tell you all my secrets." She laughed. "Besides, where do you think I've been hiding your Christmas presents all these years?"

I pretended shock. "You mean there's no Santa Claus?"

"Really, Daughter. You think I would rely on a man for something as important as your gifts?"

And I laughed, too.

"Tell the contractor to rip it all out," she said.

"You sure? Because it's kind of cool. Maybe he could add a new one?"

"It's impractical," she said. "It takes up a lot of wall space and I already have a very nice safe."

And so the vent was torn out along with the wall, and the new bedroom and huge closet were completed without a hiding niche.

Or were they?

I check every air handler. I open the panels and pull out the filters. I crawl up inside the ones big enough, coughing at the dust layered like gray ash on the metal tubes. There's a ladder in the garage and it takes me a while to get it inside, banging it against kitchen cupboards and then dinging my shin so hard that I scream "Shithelldamn!"

After I'm able to stand again, I decide to adopt shithelldamn as the official new curse of Grace Marie Pierce. It has a nice ring to it. I use the ladder and a screwdriver I also found in the garage to loosen vents near the ceiling. I try to picture Mom on a ladder, hiding secret papers or a key to a safe-deposit box. I know if that's what was required, she would have been up here in a heartbeat—wearing four-inch heels and a pencil skirt while she did it.

If my calculations are correct, I've spent about fourteen hours of every day thinking about what happened. That's over a period of sixty-five days, which means I've given this nine hundred and ten hours of thought. I've come up with two theories.

One: Someone is blackmailing Mom. My best guess is the new accountant, because how convenient that he tries to pin it on her. Maybe he'd discovered accounting discrepancies or mistakes on filing reports. Something damning enough that he could force her to divert funds rather than lose the business.

Two: Someone is threatening Mom. I've done research and I've read about Ponzi schemes, how sometimes—most of the time—they're not schemes at all. Someone started a fund and then got into some trouble. So maybe during a downturn in the market, Mom needed money to meet investor demands. Rather than default, she tried to borrow her way out. She never meant to get behind, but she did, and the moneylenders threatened to hurt her if she didn't keep paying. That would also explain her need for new investors and new money. . . . It would explain her moving the money for better returns.

In both scenarios, she was working it out. But then she got the FBI letter and that brought on the stroke.

I just need to find the proof.

The electrical boxes are next. There are fuse boxes in the garage that I remember from the last storm we had. A power surge tripped the fuses and Mom showed me how to check the box and click the levers to On. I know they have to be real because the power came back, but I run my fingers along every edge just in case.

It doesn't have to be a big space. Just enough room to hide a key to a safe-deposit box or a thumb drive with records.

The intercom has four panels. Two upstairs and two downstairs. The system was here when we moved in but I don't remember ever using it. I pull off the housing, check for a false front.

It's dusk when I do another walk-through, trailing my fingers over the stucco of each wall, playing a game with myself where I can't lose touch as I go from room to room to room.

Then I'm in Mom's closet.

My heart hitches.

My skin goes cold.

The alarm panel.

30

August

Blue Lakes is a 6.8-mile trail that winds through the Uncompahgre National Forest to a series of three lakes. It's a popular trail, a day hike described as "spectacular." I can expect to see beautiful wildflowers and towering aspens. There will be snow on the peaks and possibly muddy trails from snowmelt—this is a glacial basin, after all. I read that, too. And somewhere in this forested area there are mountain lions and black bears. I've even read about the logbook that's stationed just a few feet from the beginning of the trail.

It's a metal stand, a weathered copper color, and the rusty lid is heavy and creaks as I lift it. Inside is a pen and a logbook with pages full of names and the date and time each hiker began. I try to imagine Mom standing in this spot with the pen in her hand and the book opened to a dirt-smudged page. Did she sign or did someone sign for her?

Was she really ever here?

She told me she hiked with her friend Suzanne from college. I called Suzanne from college in June. I found an old photo with four women posed behind a banner that read CAMPUS YOUNG REPUBLICANS. Mom stood on the far left wearing a beautiful cream sweater and dark jeans. Suzanne stood beside her with feathered hair and a scarf looped around her neck. It took a while but I found Suzanne through the Internet and when I explained who I was, she said, "I'm so very sorry" and "How is your mother?" and "I'm sure she'll clear it all up just as soon as she recovers." When I asked her about the hikes, she said it wasn't her. They'd been friends in college but had drifted apart. "It must have been another Suzanne," she said. "Must have been," I agreed. Gullible as I am, I believed it.

I sign the book now, a record of what I'm not sure.

Grace Pierce and Shadow
TIME: 12:11 p.m.

Cecily once told me that if you see the numbers 11:11 you should make a wish. That it means angels are with you. I wonder if 12:11 is significant. Or does it just mean that the angels were here an hour ago and I've missed them?

The dirt is a disappointed gray and full of gravel as I start up the trail. It cuts between a stream on my left and a heavily wooded slope to the right. Tall grasses grow along the trail, scratching my arms. I'm glad I'm wearing pants.

With each step, buzzy things flutter around me and I swat them away, wondering if they're bothering Sam or if even they know better.

Neither of us has said anything since we started walking. I feel like I've already said too much. Sam has retreated into himself and I'm trying to do the same. Mostly, I'm just trying to fill my lungs with oxygen. It doesn't take long for the trail to slope up. We're not even at the top of the first hill and my quads are burning and there's an answering ache in my lungs. Phoenix is at sea level and this is definitely not Phoenix.

My heart is pumping and I use the excuse of taking off my jacket to catch my breath. As I wad up the coat and stuff it in my pack, Sam waits, one hand threaded around the strap of his pack, one leg forward, his shaggy hair somehow perfectly mussed like some damn model for Timberland. He's not even breathing hard. On the other hand, I'm sticky with grime, my hair feels like straw, and I'm starting to wonder if I can handle this physically. I've always been in good shape. Golf isn't high intensity but you get a workout walking eighteen holes pulling a cart of metal clubs. But I haven't played since the spring and I haven't done much more than ride my bike to the bus stop and walk the aisles of Circle K for Diet Cokes and Skittles.

Skittles are heavy with beta-carotenes. That's what makes them orange and green.

Cecily used to say that. I suppose she still does.

"Hey!"

My eyes flash open—I didn't realize I'd closed them. Sam is watching me, one hand out, as if he's afraid I'll fall. "You . . . okay?"

"Fine." Even that one word is thready with exhaustion. "I'm just used to more oxygen in the air." I start moving again, lifting my feet over rocks embedded in the path.

"So why didn't you ever come with your mom?"

"She started coming before I was born, and then, I don't know. I was too little, I guess. And by the time I got older, it had become a place for her to get away."

"Get away from what?"

"I'll add that to the list," I say, "of all the questions that will never be answered."

A bird calls from somewhere above, squawking until another bird answers. Wings flutter through the trees and I imagine a mom calling her baby home for lunch.

I turn when the trail turns and climb a few steps into cool shadow. Up ahead a log blocks the path. It's black with damp, limbs poking out in interesting angles. My feet slow and my hands rise—thumbs touching, pointer fingers making goalposts to form a camera frame. If I'd come across this spot four months ago, I would have waited for the sun to rise a little more and then angled the shot, mirroring the fingers of branches with fingers of sunlight.

Something clicks by my ear and when I look over, Sam is crouched beside me, his own camera steady in his hand.

"You really do have your camera."

"Always."

I didn't think I could feel worse, but I'm wrong again. Sam's camera is an older-model Canon, and I don't guess he'll have a better one now. He stands and puts the lens cap on and then stows it in his pack.

"Will you tell me how you got that shot from last semester? The ghosted image of the man on the park bench. Did you shoot the foreground separately and then combine them in post?"

"No." He resettles the pack over his shoulders.

The log is too wide to step over, so I sit on it and swing my legs over. "An ND filter to blur motion?"

"Nope."

My pant leg catches on a branch and I scrape my hand pulling myself free. "You didn't do it by varying shutter speeds—I tried."

"You tried?" He hops on top of the log and lightly comes down on the trail.

A blush crawls up my neck. "I don't understand why it's a big secret." I'm still trying to wipe the sting from my hand along with the dirt and chips of bark. "Why don't you just tell me?"

"Why should I?"

"So you can prove how much better you are."

"I don't need to prove anything to you."

I scoff loudly, filling one breath of air with as much disgust as I can manage. "Say what you want, but I know I did good work in class." I think about how I ran to Cecily's the morning after my mom's stroke. How much I wanted the photo of my mom to be entered in the school competition. "Maybe the photo I turned in would never have won. But there's no way to know that now. Would you like to know why?"

He turns away, starting up the trail. He doesn't want to hear. He doesn't want to know. Why would he? People only care about pain if it's their own. But that day, that moment, was one of the worst in a list of very bad days and very bad moments.

I can still hear my indrawn breath when the doorbell rang that afternoon. Can feel the wariness that made me hesitate and check through the glass in the front door. I saw no one when I looked, only an envelope propped against a column. I wouldn't have opened it—I'd gotten smart by then. But this was a gold interoffice manila envelope exactly like the ones we used at Desert Sky. The ones we were given by Mr. Dean to submit our contest entries.

It's strange the things I remember: the heat of the travertine beneath my bare feet, the strains of a Taylor Swift song that drifted from a car passing by, the rough feel of the envelope in my hands. And when I opened it, I remember the way my chest caved in, how I arced into the pain. How I still couldn't contain it.

And there was no one to tell. No one who would care.

All of that floods through me again. My anger centers on Sam. He can damn well listen to me now. "I said," I repeat loudly, "do you want to know why?" I jog to catch up, ignoring the sting of my boots rubbing against my heels.

"My photo was returned to me. Torn up into neat little strips."

His long strides never waver, as if I'm nothing more than one of the pesky mosquitoes constantly buzzing around us. "Did you hear me?" I shout. "That was my photo. My work. And yes, I know everyone has lost a lot, but that should have been separate. That was the only good thing I had, and it was stolen from me by some coward. Some asshole who didn't even have the decency to face me."

I'm breathless trying to keep up with Sam. "Do you hear me?"

I tug on his arm and when he turns, his eyes are blazing. "Don't tell me about what was stolen from you."

My jaw drops. I reel back. He's angry—that I expect. But he isn't surprised. I can see it in his face. "You . . . you *knew*? You did, didn't you?" He looks away but I shove at his arm. "Tell me how? Who told you?"

"Nobody told me." He pivots to face me, planting himself in the middle of the trail. "I was the one who put the envelope by your front door."

"You?" Once when I was little, I ran into a sliding glass door. I was shocked when I hit it. I'd never even seen it. I feel that way now. Before I can draw another breath, something flashes from the corner of my eye.

The tall grass parts and a bear charges through, heading right for us.

31

August

I scream as a black blur lurches onto the trail. My arm flies up in defense as I drop to the dirt.

"It's okay, it's okay!"

Sam's voice—calm and kind. But he's not talking to me. When I open my eyes, he's crouched beside me, his hands rubbing at the enormous head of a panting, drooling dog.

Sam shoots me a weird look, and I realize I'm still cowering. I lower my arm but my knees refuse to straighten. I sit in the dirt instead. Adrenaline is still pumping through my veins, making me jittery. "I thought it was a bear."

Jogging up the trail is a girl with short black hair streaked with blue and the bone structure of a French perfume model. She's wearing hiking shorts, boots, and a sleeveless tank with no bra. Her gaze skims past me, and her smile blooms when she sees Sam.

"Afternoon," she says. Her shoulders shift back so her

lack of a bra is even more apparent. *Those will be down to your knees by the time you're thirty,* I want to tell her. But what do I care about her breasts? Maybe Sam loves sagging breasts, in which case he can follow her and her freaking dog down the trail. I climb to my feet, brushing off dirt. He's still rubbing at the dog's wiry hair. It looks like buffalo hair. I wrinkle my nose. It smells exactly like I imagine a buffalo would smell.

"You met Dandy," she says with a grin.

"He jumped me," I snap. "He's not on a leash." I'm shaking like a crazy person, but I don't really care. A girl should be able to climb a mountain before she unplugs her mother without getting jumped by a dog. I mean, really. Is that so much to ask? My breath comes in short, sharp gasps. *Oh God, I am unhinged.*

"We're not real big on rules out here." She looks to Sam like he's her new confidant and they can bond over my insanity. "Dandy likes to be sociable."

"Sociable? He nearly ripped off my arm."

"She," the girl corrects. "And she's sweet as marmalade, aren't you, Dandy?" She crouches by Sam, who is now rubbing the beast's pointy ears.

"She a Lab mix?" Sam asks.

"We're not sure. She was a rescue dog."

When the dog licks at his neck, I've had enough. Enough of the dog. Enough of the girl. Enough of Sam smiling and flirting when he's just admitted he's the biggest piece of shit on the planet.

"Well, nice to meet you," I lie to the girl. I turn to Sam. "You should stay. You and Dandy seem to be developing a special bond."

He rises slowly. "But you and I have such a special bond ourselves."

"Not all that special," I snap. "You don't have my drool on your neck."

"Are you offering?"

His gaze holds mine, and more heat washes through my cheeks. "I hate you," I say in a conversational voice.

"I'm aware." Then he bends over the dog. "Bye, gorgeous."

Gorgeous?

Braless Babe looks confused and disappointed. Exactly like Dandy, in fact.

I turn to the trail and throw every bit of energy into moving my feet. My blood has to be 213 degrees right now, because it's boiling. The trail takes a right turn around some trees and I swipe at a stray branch hanging over the path.

Sam falls in behind me. "You going to freak out at every dog?"

"That dog was the size of a horse."

"Its tail was wagging."

"I didn't see tail. I saw teeth."

"You just have to learn to read the signs. Especially up here, where everyone's got a dog. Are their ears up or down? Tail wagging or tucked low? Shoulders forward or back? It's not like with people. A dog's body language never lies."

"You think I care about the shoulders of a dog?" I spin to face him. "How could you hate me so much?" Tears spring to my eyes and I'm angry at my own weakness. When do I stop feeling so much pain? "Were you the one who shredded the photo, too?"

"No!" He shoves his fingers through his hair. "No," he repeats, softer as if the word is pulled from somewhere deeper. His gaze ranges over the trees and down toward the stream. "Mr. Dean shredded the photo. He did it during class right after the FBI confiscated the top-of-the-line photo printer your mom donated."

"In front of the whole class? And no one said anything?"

"Nearly everyone in that class lost something in the Fund. Including Mr. Dean, whose wife is on dialysis and was depending on that money." His gaze fixes on mine. "What did you expect us to do? Your mother swindled everyone. Were we supposed to celebrate her picture?"

Pain throbs against my temples. "Congratulations," I say. "You figured out the perfect way to get your revenge."

"Grace—"

I turn away but he reaches for my arm, stopping me. "Would you listen?"

Sighing, I push the damp hair off my forehead. "Listen to what, Sam? Or should I read your body language, see what your shoulders are saying? When you set that envelope down, were they pushed back with pride over how much you were going to hurt me? How good it would feel to get back at me?"

"That's not what—"

"That's exactly what you did," I interrupt. "You purposely left it there so I would know." I take off, moving as fast as my tired legs allow, because the only way this ends is for me to get to the top. I've only gone a few yards when my foot skids on loose rock. Before I go down, Sam catches me, steadying me with his hand.

I yank free, crying, "Don't touch me."

"Just . . . take it easy."

"Don't tell me to take it easy. What does that even mean?"

"I don't know. It doesn't mean shit."

I gasp for air. My lungs feel like balloons that won't inflate.

"You're hyperventilating. Put your head between your knees."

"Don't tell me what I'm doing." And then I put my head between my knees because if I don't I might pass out.

It's quiet for a minute and then two. The dark spots in front of my eyes finally fade and my breathing begins to feel normal.

"I put it there so you would know," he says. His voice is as gravelly as the ground beneath me. "So you could submit another one or file a complaint. So you could do whatever the hell you wanted to do. I did it so you would know."

His eyes flash with conflicting emotions I can't begin to understand. I can't even understand how I'm feeling myself, except a little stunned. And a little like a candle that burned out and has been relit. "Sam—" My voice is hesitant and I'm not sure what I mean to say. But he stops me with a hand, and whatever he's feeling has been wiped from his face, shuttered behind cold eyes.

"Don't," he says. "I did what I thought was right, but your mother is still a thief. For all I know, so are you."

He brushes by me, moving intently up the trail.

I shake my head and sigh as a bank of gray clouds drifts into view. "You're right," I murmur to myself. "I can't read dogs or people."

32

July

The mechanism works exactly the way I expect.

It wasn't hard to find, either. The alarm panel isn't big—the size of a 14 x 18 print. The outer door opens with a flick of my thumb. It all looks so real inside. There are tiny fuses all numbered with white stickers. Yellow, red, and blue wires run like veins across the panel. It's a work of art. I wonder if that's what the person who constructed it thought. I wonder if that's how they spend their days—making fake things. Did Mom go online? "Fake Fuses 'R' Us."

There's a small bump in the inner wall. A spring, I think, though I'm not really mechanical.

If I press it . . . I lean my head against the wall, weak with relief. My heart is racing. This is the proof I've been searching for—it has to be. She left this here, where I would be the one to find it. My hands tremble when I press the button.

There's a metallic click and then the panel pops open. I curl my fingers in the gap and open the door. The space is rectangular and deep, finished with white paint. It smells a little musty, but it's clean of dust. There's a beautiful backpack, black with gray pockets and straps. When I pull it out, I can feel the padding along one zippered side. A camera bag! I tug at the zipper and the face of a camera gleams up at me, carefully tucked in a compartment and flanked by a long lens. A new Leica camera! The one I've been salivating over for months. I hug the pack close.

Then I see a large manila envelope.

My breath catches. I lift it gingerly, hardly believing that it's in my hands. Finally. I know it's the evidence I need to clear Mom's name and lead the FBI to the missing money. I can fix this—fix everything.

With a long exhale, I slide a finger under the flap of the envelope and gently tear it open.

33

August

The next hour passes in a haze. I focus on my feet, on putting one in front of the other. The clouds have drifted in closer, darker, and at first I'm only aware of it as a vague feeling of shade. It feels nice. Then the rock in my shoe finds a spot just under my arch and I have to stop.

Sam waits while I untie my boot and shake out a handful of pebbles. He takes out a water bottle and squeezes a stream into his mouth. As he clicks the mouthpiece down, he asks, "You have water, don't you?"

"Yes."

"You want me to get it out for you?"

Do I want him going into my backpack? "No." I bounce on one foot, wobbling as I shove the shoe back on. Then I pull out the bottle I've been refilling since Phoenix. "You're not even breathing hard, are you?"

"We've only hiked about three miles."

Uncapping my bottle, I look around. "Three miles? We can't have gone that far." I shuffle my feet in a half-circle and wince. My heels hurt and there's a spot where my little toe is rubbing against the boot. And something has started itching on my left ankle in a way that makes me want to rub up against the roughest-looking tree bark I can find. The valley has opened up around us. The trees are still thick to my right but the trail has leveled out into a meadow filled with wildflowers. It's beautiful.

And it's all wrong.

"We can't be three miles in. We would be higher." I study the vein of the trail stretching in front of us and a sinking sensation grows in the pit of my empty stomach. "This doesn't look right."

"I thought you'd never been?"

"I haven't, but the Internet said we're supposed to be going up."

"We did for a while."

"But it's supposed to be mostly up. Strenuous up."

"I wouldn't call this strenuous."

"Plus, it's a popular trail and we haven't seen anyone since that girl and her rabid pony."

He slides his hands into the pockets of his jeans. "You're just thinking of that now?"

Above us, the branches of a tree sway in the wind and leaves scatter down. The darkness finally registers as more than shade. "Storm clouds." Quickly, I tuck my bottle away. "We should go back."

"What do you mean go back?"

"We must have missed a turn."

He quirks an eyebrow. "We?"

"You weren't invited on this trip," I snap. "You can go home any time you like."

The trees above shudder again. Must be more wind. Except. I swallow. I don't feel any wind down here.

"If you tell me where we're headed, I can keep us on the right trail."

"There must have been a turnoff near where we saw the girl and her dog." Rocks skitter down the hill and I glance up. Now I see why the trees were moving. "Speaking of," I say, relieved that we're not alone out here after all. "There's that dog again."

Sam follows my gaze. "Grace." His voice is a choked whisper. A furry black shape emerges through the trees. "That's not a dog. That's a bear."

34

August

My heart stops, then jump-starts with panic. I scurry back, tripping over my own feet and falling hard on my butt and my hands. I try to push myself up, but my shoes slide in the loose leaves and my hands feel as brittle as the twigs on the trail. Sam grabs my arm and pulls me up. The bear hardly seems to be moving, but it's covering ground fast as it lumbers down the hillside toward the trail.

Toward us.

I've never seen a bear before. Not one that wasn't behind an enclosure in a zoo. It's huge, its legs swinging in powerful sweeping motions as bushes crumble and rocks dance out of its way.

"Get back," Sam orders. He stands in front of me, his arm stretched out like a barrier. My hands are on his pack, my fingers digging into the material. "Stay quiet. Maybe it won't bother with us."

The bear's head swings our way, and it pauses, its nose lifting. Sniffing.

Oh God. My heart pounds hard against my ribs as the bear drops onto the trail, only a hundred yards or so from us. The smell overpowers me. It's like a big garbage barrel in Phoenix that's been sitting in the sun for a week.

"Sam." My throat is hardening into concrete. "What do we do? Do we run?"

"We can't outrun a bear."

"Then what do we do?"

"We don't panic."

"What else?" I grip tighter to his pack. "What else do we do?"

We're still moving back, one slow step at a time.

The bear shuffles toward us. The claws. *Oh God.* I squeeze my eyes shut.

"We make noise," he says suddenly. "That's what we do. Lots of noise. The bear wants food, not a fight."

But we are food.

"All right?" he asks.

My hands search for a better hold, shifting from his backpack to the sleeve of his shirt, to the flexed muscle of his bicep. "All right."

"All right?" he says again. Louder.

"All right." My voice wobbles. I try again, crying, "All right!"

"All right?" he yells. "All fucking right!"

The bear rears up and I scream, stumbling back.

"Run, Grace," Sam shouts. "Run hard!" Then he strides forward and throws his hands in the air, as if he's waving at the bear. "Help!" he yells. "Fire!"

I start up the slope, reaching for the roots of bushes, pulling hard to propel myself up the incline to the thick trunk of a tree. When I turn to look, Sam has a stick and he's waving it in front of him, gripped tight in two hands like a sword. "Get away!" He bangs the stick on a tree. Dirt and leaves fly up and the bear is still there, but he's stopped moving.

"It's working. It's— Keep screaming," I say. "Shoo!" I yell at the bear. I bend down for a rock and throw it as hard as I can. "SHOO, BEAR! SHOO!"

The bear rolls its head my way, rising on its back legs. Sam darts forward, waving the branch and screaming. "Go on—get!"

That seems to decide something for the bear. It drops down to its four legs and ambles back a few paces. Then it continues down the hillside, sniffing as it goes.

Crying out in relief, I slump against the tree.

"Come on," Sam says. He runs to me and holds out a hand. I half skid down the ten feet I've climbed and grab hold. My feet wobble but he grips me tightly, bearing my weight until my shoes hit the flat trail again.

Then he says, "Run."

■ ■ ■

We run until I can't breathe. Until the sweat is slick across my skin and every bit of my blood feels as if it's pounding through my ears. Until I'm only a swollen heart and lungs like tattered balloons.

When I finally trip over a tree root and go down, Sam is there, helping me up again. "It's okay," I pant. "I'm okay."

"I think we're safe." He's breathless, too. "I think we lost it."

I nod, more blood rushing to my head as I bend over my knees and take in as much air as I can. My legs are like jelly. I rest my hands on my thighs and then gasp at the pain. When I look at my left hand, the center of my palm is scraped red.

"You all right?"

"I hurt myself," I say dumbly. "I don't remember when."

"Come on. Let's sit over here." He points to a boulder buried in the mountainside just a few feet farther.

Nodding, I move with him, and it's nearly all I can do to reach the boulder. I'm shaking but I'm also rigid, as if every muscle is stiff as bone and every bone as loose as muscle. I sink down, and when he settles beside me, I'm glad. I pretend to shift for a more comfortable spot, but really I move until I can feel the barest pressure of his knee. His arm is a solid wall, his fingers only inches from my own, and I want to lean even closer. A breath rattles loudly from his lips and then his shoulder is resting against mine. It might be me, but I think it's both of us leaning toward each other.

"Holy hell," he mutters.

"Shithelldamn," I add. He looks at me, and I shrug. "It's my new favorite curse."

"It's a good one."

I'm slowly aware that the rock we're sitting on is cold. A chill rises through me, and the sweat beading on my skin is replaced by goose bumps.

"Fire?" I say suddenly. The word springs to my lips as I picture Sam screaming at the bear.

"It's one of those safety things I learned in school. It was better than *shoo*," he adds. "'Shoo, bear, shoo?'" He rolls his eyes but he's grinning—a goofy, lopsided grin that makes me smile, too.

"I thought it was very effective," I say. "So was the whole sword routine you had going."

He ruffles a hand through his hair and leaves fall out. "Not a sword. A lightsaber. I had many hours of practice that I can now tell my mother were not a waste of time."

"I tried to throw rocks."

"I saw that," he says dryly. "The bear saw that. The bear stopped to laugh."

"It wasn't that bad." I shiver. "Did you see when he stood up? The size of his head? Those teeth? That would not have been a little nip." I shoot him a sidelong look. "And if you tell me you could read that bear's shoulders, I'm going to kick you." I swallow. "Just as soon as I have the energy to stand."

I take another look in the direction we came. Nothing is moving, though the shadows are heavier. Thicker. It's hard to see much of anything beyond our small clearing. How late is it? I check my watch and realize it isn't the time that's shifted as much as the sky. The clouds that have been gathering are a charcoal gray.

"You think it's still out there?" I ask.

"Somewhere."

I lick my lips. My mouth is as dry as the dead leaves scattered at our feet. Even as I'm thinking it, he holds out his water bottle. "Here."

"I have a bottle." But it's in my pack, and I don't think I can reach around to pull it out. "Thank you." I take a small sip, feeling the warm water ease its way down my throat. My stomach immediately feels sick. Or maybe it already did. "I shouldn't have seen *The Revenant*." I pass him back the bottle. "Did you see it?"

"Yeah."

"I didn't even watch the whole thing. I just saw the bear scene because everyone was saying you have to see it." I wipe a hand over my mouth. "I did not need to see the bear scene."

"That's why I said we should make noise."

I'm horrified. "You were going by a movie?"

"Worked, didn't it?" He leans forward and I feel untethered with his arm gone. "If it comes back, we should do what Leo DiCaprio did in the movie."

"Get our chests ripped open?"

"Play dead."

I rub my hands over my chilled arms. "You think it's coming back?"

"Probably not." He shakes his head. "Definitely not."

"Liar," I say. "You just don't want me to freak out."

"And are you?"

I check in with my racing pulse. "Kind of. I'm not really an outdoorsy person."

"Really? What a shock," he says dryly.

"I'm not that bad," I grumble. "I was a Girl Scout for two years. I even went on three mandatory camping trips. Although"—I shrug—"I was more interested in organizing the supplies."

"So we're lost on a mountain and you have no useful knowledge?"

"I can make s'mores."

"You have chocolate and marshmallows and graham crackers?"

I clear my throat. "Scratch that. I have no useful knowledge."

He slides to the end of the boulder. "You wait here. I'll take a look down the slope." He stands and I'm suddenly on my feet, too.

"No. Don't go." I brush dirt off my pants to hide my flush. "I mean, I'll go with you."

He nods, not commenting on the fact that my voice is now two octaves higher. "Stay behind me."

As if I had anything else in mind.

He turns toward the ridgeline and slowly picks his way through the trees we must have just passed. I don't recognize any of it. I wasn't looking, other than to find the next foothold. We don't go far, just past a few trees, when we come to a clearing. "I don't see anything," he says.

My jaw drops as I look at the valley below us. "I didn't realize we'd climbed so high." The sky feels closer, the clouds pressing down on us. I remember the bus driver and his announcement about rain. "Did we come up this way?" We couldn't have. A few steps farther and I'm standing at the edge of an overhang.

"We should keep moving. Get down the mountain before the storm comes."

"But the bear is down there."

The sky picks that second to crackle with a distant sound of thunder.

"Which way?" I ask.

He slowly turns, his breath sighing out. His gray shirt is half brown with dirt, and his jeans are torn at the knee. But his profile is straight and strong. He seems as resilient as the aspens that cling to the mountainside. I look away. Watching him makes me sad for things I told myself I don't want anymore.

Then he mutters a curse, and when I turn back, he's holding his cell phone. "No signal. What about yours?" he asks.

"I don't have a phone."

"What?"

"I was using a prepaid. I ran out of funds."

His eyes narrow the way I knew they would.

"It's the truth, okay? It's what happened. I'm not asking for your pity."

"You're not getting any."

My voice rises. "Then don't look at me like that."

"Like what?"

"Like I'm lying about the phone and like you just remembered that you hate me."

Another boom of thunder fills the sky, this one louder. Closer.

He buries his fingers in his hair. "There is so much to hate right now. You are just the beginning."

A vein pulses at my temple as my emotions seesaw back to anger. "You know what? This isn't exactly a trip to Happyville for me, either. And if you weren't here, I wouldn't be lost right now."

He dips his head toward me, his glare back in full force. "Come again?"

"If you hadn't distracted me, I would have stayed on the right trail and I would have climbed the mountain and there wouldn't have been a bear in my face. The bear is on you. So there—that's one thing that's not my fault. In fact, I'm going to blame you for my hand, too." I hold it up, the dirt and blood a smeared brown. "My hand is bleeding and I don't know why but it's your fault that we went flying up a mountain because it's your fault that a bear was chasing us."

The thunder booms again and the trees rustle, the leaves beginning to move with a sharper wind.

His fingers curl into white-knuckled fists. "You want to blame the storm on me, too?"

"As soon as I can figure out how, yes!"

"What about your mother? Should we blame any of

this on the fact that she's a criminal?" He jerks as lightning slices above us in a jagged arc. "We've got to get out of here. Now."

He starts moving, not waiting for an answer, and I don't give one. He shoves aside branches, forcing his way through lashing wind and whirling dust. I follow, blind to everything but the path he's taking. There are a few places where he heads down, but each time, he pulls up when the ridge ends in a drop.

"Back," he says for the third time.

"Which way?"

He returns to the small clearing we just crossed and circles it like a caged cat. We've been through here twice already. Every time we break through a gap, we end up in more dense brush and trees. No trail. No sign of a trail.

There's a loud crack from above. Heavy drops of rain splatter my face and my arm. Sam wipes at his cheek, staring at the wetness on his fingers as if he can't believe it. His expression darkens every bit as much as the sky. There's no cool exterior now. The storm is breaking from within. "Fuck!" he screams.

I brace myself. Some storms you hide from, and some storms you meet with a fury of your own.

35

August

"What the hell are we doing here?" He grabs a small boulder and hurls it at a tree. It smacks the trunk and rolls down in a shower of leaves. Then he turns his rage on me. "Is this some kind of joke, Grace? Drag me out to the middle of nowhere and get me lost, or killed by a bear?"

"I didn't ask you to come!" I cry.

"I need the money. Where is it? No more bullshit. Is it even up here?"

"I told you it wasn't."

"And I'm supposed to believe you? The face of the Family Fund? You're as much of a liar as your mother, aren't you?"

"You want money? Here." I dig into my pocket and pull out the wad of bills I offered him earlier. Coins fly out, too, burying themselves in the tall grass. "Take it." I shove the bills into his chest. "That's my money."

He fans out the few twenties. "I don't want your money. I want *my* money."

"It's gone."

"Bullshit!" He paces away and then back. Stripped of his control, he suddenly looks younger. And every bit as frightened as I am. "You don't get it, do you? My mother is waiting at home for me to bring back that money. I promised her. It's how I'm going to take care of her. It's how I can do what my brother didn't." His eyes are wild in the darkening sky. "It has to be somewhere." His gaze snags on my pack and he freezes. "You won't let that pack out of your sight, will you? Why is that, Grace? What have you got in there?"

Before I can react, he's spinning me around and tugging hard at my shoulder straps. I cry out as my arms are yanked back and then the pack is off. Sam drops to one knee, and I watch in horror as he finds the zipper for the small compartment at the bottom. My hand flies out. "No—"

He pulls out the blue bandana, takes a quick look, and shoves it back in. My heart pounds and blood beats a crazy rhythm in my head. He opens the next compartment and sets my water bottle and flashlight on the ground along with my jacket. I grab it and pull it on. He unzips the main compartment and the camera flies free, the strap dangling from his fingers. He looks at me, his mouth open and heaving. "Are you kidding me?"

"I told you I had a camera."

"This can't be it. A camera?"

I shove my things back in my pack. "Yes, a camera!"

Cursing, he slams it on a boulder and I cry out, lunging forward but it's too late. The camera body cracks.

"What are you doing? Stop! That's a thirty-thousand-dollar camera!"

His face goes white. Thunder booms from over the mountain peak. "A . . . what?"

Rain spatters in heavier drops.

"You heard me."

"Thirty thousand dollars? That's what a year of college costs—with room and board. It's . . . it's . . ."

He can't seem to finish, so I do it for him. "Yes, I know. It's an expensive camera. And I'm Janelle Pierce's daughter and that's the life I had. A thirty-thousand-dollar camera that she bought for me with money she stole from the people I introduced her to."

He straightens, wiping rain from his face. Thunder rolls like a wave across the valley. "You knew."

"I didn't."

"You did." His head shakes as he moves closer. "You almost had me fooled. You know that? I thought maybe you were a victim, too. But you knew exactly what you were selling every time you told someone about the Family Fund." He holds up the shattered camera. "How did you manage to keep this from the FBI, Grace? Where did it come from? Where was it hidden and what was hidden with it?"

"I don't have to tell you anything!"

"Did. You. Know?" His shout echoes with the thunder.

Then the sky cracks open and so do I. "Yes!" I scream back. "Yes. I knew!"

36

August

Lightning explodes above us, illuminating Sam's face. His expression is one of horror. Disgust. I let my tears fall as I wait for him to curse me again. To walk away. To run. I would run from myself if I could.

Another boom of thunder jars us both. It's getting closer.

"We need to find cover," he yells.

The rain is coming down harder. Sam points to a pine tree, the branches swaying like arms warning us away. "We'll make a shelter under there. Use the tree for cover. Find branches."

"Go down," I cry. "You'll make it without me."

His voice lashes out at me. "Branches, Grace. Now!"

The wind is howling through my head. The words I threw at him still burn on my tongue. I've held them in for so long, hoping that Mom would wake up and explain. That somehow she wouldn't be a monster and neither would I.

"Grace!" he shouts. "I need your help."

I blink my lashes clear of rain and tears. He's already dragging a heavy limb toward the tree, a few branches still attached with leaves that sweep the ground like a broom.

Help. I can help. The thought gets me moving. I climb into the brush and hunt through the muck for the end of another downed limb. I tug, tensing my back and legs against the heavy wood. My feet skid in the new mud. I twist the branch under my arms, pulling as hard as I can. Then Sam is beside me, his legs bent and his thighs straining. The branch shifts and he goes down, then scrambles up. He drops his head and yanks again and together we drag it to the tree. I gasp for air as he balances it against the trunk, using the branches to create a wall of leaves.

"More," he shouts. "Smaller branches to fill in the spaces."

I stumble back toward the bushes, the storm pounding around me and through me. I fill my arms with broken branches and leaves. I carry them back to Sam.

"Your jacket." His voice is as stinging as the rain.

"What?"

"Is that Gore-Tex? Is that a twenty-thousand-dollar jacket?" His hand is out. "Give it to me."

I struggle with the sleeves, realizing that the fabric is repelling the rain. I don't know what the jacket is worth. It's worth more than I am. I hand it to him, and the rain spreads new cold over my neck and back, immediately soaking my T-shirt.

He lays the jacket on top of the shelter. I watch as he ties down the sleeves but in my mind I'm seeing myself bring bagels to the staff lounge at Desert Sky. Passing out Mom's business cards to the teachers willing to listen to my practiced pitch.

Thunder booms directly overhead. Something cracks and the ground shudders.

"Get under the shelter!" Sam cries.

I tilt my face to the sky. Lift my arms. I feel pagan. Ancient. I'm washed in sin and the storm is my justice.

A tree branch cracks above. I watch it crash down, landing so close leaves scrape my bare arm.

"You have a death wish?" Sam screams.

"Maybe I do!" I scream back.

"Get in the shelter, Grace!"

Another shaft of lightning splinters the sky. He lunges for me, pulling me down.

"Let go of me!"

"No!" He half drags, half carries me to the small lean-to.

"You heard me. I knew! I knew what she was doing and I helped her."

He ducks under the branches and pulls me with him, not letting go until I'm on my knees, shaking and sobbing.

"Are you listening to me?"

He shifts in the tiny space, twisting me with him, and I use his shoulder as a brace until I'm sitting on my bottom.

"Yes," he says. "I'm listening. I heard every word." He leans out into the storm and pulls our packs in. When his hand brushes mine, he curses. "You're freezing."

"I'm not." But his words waken my brain to the fact that, yes, I am freezing. My teeth start to chatter.

He takes my fingers between his palms and rubs heat into them.

"What are you doing?" I jerk away.

He says nothing but reaches for my hand again, his hold firm.

His gentleness unravels what little control I have left. My words are coated with the salt of my tears. "I lied. I'm a cheat. A thief—"

"Quiet." He blows warm air over my fingers.

I sob harder. I don't understand this. I don't understand him. He doesn't say anything else, just lets me cry, eventually switching to my other hand and warming those fingers, too.

The storm is leaking in, the rain pattering down the leafy walls and pooling on the ground. Through the opening I can see flashes of lightning but the wind is quieter in here. Finally, I regain some control and pull my hands away. I wipe at my face and take a few shuddering breaths.

"She told me times were tight," I say. "The markets weren't good. She said we needed new investors." My teeth are still chattering and I pause to catch my breath again. "I'm not even sure whose idea it was for me to transfer schools. If she brought it up or if I did. I was just so happy that I'd found a way to help."

He unzips his backpack and pulls out his sweatshirt. "Here."

I strain to read his features in the dark. "Sam, why aren't

you hearing me? I knew the Fund was in trouble and I purposely looked for new investors."

"Just take the sweatshirt."

"No." I push it back to him. "Don't be kind to me."

"Did you know what she was doing with the money?"

"I should have known. If things were so bad with the markets, then why were we doing so well? I never bothered to ask. What does that make me?"

He sets the sweatshirt in my lap. "Someone who trusted her mother."

My stomach cramps with guilt. "I thought I was doing a good thing. I thought I was Galadriel from *Lord of the Rings*. Remember the scene where she gives Frodo the light? I thought that was me. I thought I was going to be the light in places where all other lights have gone out." I twist his sweatshirt around my hands. "Go ahead," I say. "Laugh at me. Tell me what an idiot I am."

"You're an idiot, Grace. Now put on the sweatshirt."

His voice is gruff, but also kind. *How can he be kind to me?*

I slide my hands inside his sweatshirt and even though it's wet in spots, it feels so good. It envelops me and I wad the extra material in my fists, warming my cheeks with it. "You should have left me out there. I'm the one who told you to invest."

"You weren't."

I shake my head, hardly hearing him. "I'm the reason you've lost everything."

"No. You're not." His voice is so low I almost don't hear him. "I lost everything way before the Family Fund."

The wind moans through the leaves above us. "You mean Marcus?"

He folds his arms around his knees. His shirt is soaked wet against his skin but when he shivers I don't think it's from the cold. "You asked me earlier if I knew what he was doing. I did. I knew all about it and I didn't stop what happened. I guess that makes us both monsters."

Thunder shakes the ground and lightning flares from the opening in our shelter. The world is suddenly visible. It's only a flash—too quick to really see. But enough to know there's more out there than you realized.

37

August

The storm is overhead now. Above us, my jacket flaps as the rain continues. Branches skitter past the opening of our lean-to, bouncing off trees and splitting apart. It feels like that could be me, loose in the storm and spinning out of control. I would be, if not for Sam.

I pull my knees in and wrap my arms around them. The tent is not much bigger than the two of us, and we're hunched in the narrow space, the leaves poking from the sides, the bark of the tree just behind us. But it's shelter. It's a roof over our heads, even if it's just leaves. It makes me think of the shelter I've been trying to build for myself since the day the FBI announced its investigation. A flimsy one, made of rationalizations, blind trust, and the mantra *When my mom wakes up* . . . For months I hid under it all, trying to convince myself I was safe. Now here I am, in the middle of an actual storm, and in some strange way I do feel safe. I feel at peace. I've been through the worst—braved the lightning and the truth—and I'm still here.

Sam is still here.

I don't want to read too much into that—I know he's after the money. But for the first time in a very long time, I don't feel alone. As long as it continues to storm, there's nowhere for us to go. Nothing for us to find.

Or not find.

"Will you tell me about him?" I ask. "About Marcus?"

Sam tenses.

"I just mean . . . tell me about *him*. What was he like?"

He's quiet for a long time. I listen to the rain and the fading thunder. I wonder if Sam can taste mint on the air the way I do.

"I don't know," he says. "He was just Marcus."

He hands me his water bottle, but I don't take it. "It's okay. You're almost out."

"We'll put it outside and collect the rainwater."

"Oh." I take a big swallow and give it back.

He turns it around in his hands. "Marcus was big. Everything about him. His size. His laugh. Go big or go home. That was my brother."

A crackle of light spreads from beyond the treetops and I can see stars now that the clouds have shifted. Sam finishes the water and then leans out of the shelter, flattening a spot in the mud and grinding the bottle into it so it's steady. I hand him my own empty bottle and he sets it beside his. He pulls back in, rain dripping from his hair.

"Were you a Boy Scout?"

"I watch a lot of survival shows." He wipes his muddy hands on his jeans and it makes me wonder what he was like as a kid.

"Did you have freckles?"

"What?"

"Freckles. When you were little?"

"I don't know. Maybe."

"I only had one." I tilt my head to show him a freckle up high on my neck. It's dark, though, so I don't think he can see it. I don't know why I'm showing him. "It would be nice to be a kid again." I sigh, wanting my memory to take me back to something good, something easy. "So what were you like?"

"Me? I was just a kid."

"What kind of a kid?"

"A dumb one."

But he says it with a smile, resting his chin on one bent knee. "I didn't care about school, except for recess. I played whatever sport I could, even though I wasn't talented like Marcus was. I loved motorbikes. We had an old Kawasaki dirt bike that we were fixing up together. We'd take it out in the desert. Usually, Marcus would ride and I'd catch lizard tails until he came back."

"Lizard tails?"

"It's a survival thing. If some lizards get caught, they shed their tails."

"That's awful."

"They grow back."

"I know, but still."

He grins. "I got seven one time. Even Marcus was impressed. He put two up his nose and two in his ears. It was sick. It was totally sick and we laughed our asses off."

His memories warm me. I imagine I can hear an echo of Sam and Marcus laughing in the wind that's beginning to soften. A sigh rises in my chest and I can't believe I feel this . . . *okay.*

"I never had a brother or a sister," I say. "But I always wanted one. I wanted a big family like you see on TV where everyone is fighting over the bathroom sink and drawing straws for the last brownie."

"Marcus and I wrestled."

"Over brownies?"

"Over everything."

"And by wrestling I assume you mean throwing each other over couches and rolling around the carpet in a headlock?"

His teeth gleam white. "Exactly."

"I've seen that on TV, too."

"You've never experienced a good headlock? I can show you."

"No thanks," I say dryly. But I'm smiling. "I think I would rather be the judge of a wrestling match."

"No judges in wrestling. Referees."

"Do referees get whistles? I always liked whistles. I used to have a yellow one for playgroup."

"You had a whistle?"

"It was the only way to organize everyone."

"I thought you said it was a playgroup?"

"Well, yes. But I had very good ideas for group activities."

He makes a noise that sounds like something between a laugh and a bark.

"Are you making fun of me?"

"Yes."

His grin is so unexpected . . . so beautiful.

"Were you always so serious about everything?" he asks.

"I wasn't serious. I was organized."

"I can picture exactly how you were. Full of rules and very . . . earnest."

"That makes me sound like someone's uncle." I shift on the wet ground, exchanging one bruised spot for another. "I wasn't earnest. I was fun. I would make up plays and assign everyone a role."

"Uh-huh," he says, sounding unconvinced. "And if kids didn't obey, did you blow your whistle at them?"

"You would have been assigned the role of the bad guy."

"No," he says, his grin widening. "I would have stolen your whistle."

"My favorite yellow whistle?" I glare in mock outrage. "I would have chased you for it, and I would have caught you because I was very fast in those days."

"And if you caught me," he says, "you would have experienced your first headlock."

I laugh—a burst of sound that I try to cover with one

hand. It's out of place here, startling and so loud I immediately feel awkward. I shouldn't be laughing. *How can I be laughing? How can I be happy?*

Sam's shoulder stiffens against mine and with just that bit of movement, reality rushes back. My own muscles shrink and pull, drawing me into myself. It's as if we both got too close to a fire and only just realized the danger. There's nowhere to move, but I can feel the distance grow between us.

My heart aches. I want to feel close to someone again. To laugh, to share stories, to like someone and have them like me, too.

It's not fair that the past can have the power to steal the present.

In the awkward stillness, the air settles heavily around my shoulders. "I think I would have liked you," I say. "From before." I picture the boy in the photo, standing apart at the side of his brother's grave. I pull Sam's sweatshirt closer around myself. "Do you think it's ever possible to go back? To be the person you once were?"

"No." He sighs. "We're not like lizards. Our tails don't grow back."

38

August

I must have fallen asleep.

I wake up, slowly aware of random things. Something hard under my shoulder. Dripping sounds—a faucet just barely on. Warmth. Weight. Slow breathing. A heart beating. *Not my heart.*

My eyes flutter open. Not a log beneath my shoulder. An arm.

I shift, turning from my side to my back, propping my weight on my elbows.

Sam shifts beside me, his arm pulling away. It's dark outside, the world reduced to shapes. And my embarrassment.

"Sorry," I mumble.

"It's okay. Not a lot of room."

"Did I . . ." I think I remember his shoulder. Or maybe his lap. *Oh God.* "I'm sorry," I say again. I sit all the way up and put as much space between us as I can. I still feel where we were touching. It's like my body has memorized the sensation and is playing it back to me. How long has it been since someone has touched me? Was it Gabe at the hospital just before he asked me about the money? *No.* He didn't touch me then. Cecily? Cecily when she slapped me?

It sounds like the rain has stopped. But there are other noises—rustlings and cracking, a low hum that might be wind or might be running water in the distance. And it's cold. Very cold. "What time is it?"

"Four. Maybe five. My phone doesn't work up here, and even if it did, the battery is dead."

He shifts again, bumping the branch wall. Water sprinkles down, the drops icy on my face. Something thuds and I wonder if we've lost part of our structure.

Remembering the flashlight in my pack, I get it out and the LED powers on with a flare of white light. It cuts through the gloom but gives only a tunnel view to the world. Our shelter is still holding, but just barely. Sam pulls in the water bottles and hands me mine. It's full again.

"Why bring a flashlight if you didn't expect to spend the night?"

"I wasn't really planning. It was there on my desk." I set the flashlight on the ground where it can provide a little light without blinding us. I sniff at my water. "I used to take it with me in case I needed to light a shot."

He takes a drink from his bottle and I watch.

"You waiting to see if I keel over and die?"

"Well"—I shrug—"you hear about things like acid rain."

"You waited to mention that until after I drank?" He takes another sip and makes a face. "It's not acid, but it does taste like dirt."

I try a sip and he's right. But I'm thirsty, and though I'd like to drink more, I take just a few swallows. I don't know when I'll be able to refill it.

"I tried light painting with a flashlight once," he says.

"Really?" I tease. "I bet you were good at it, too, with your *advanced lightsaber* skills."

"Hey, I saved you from a bear, didn't I?"

"Leo DiCaprio saved me."

"That guy? He got mauled."

I smile. "So what happened with the flashlight photos?"

"Found something more interesting."

"And you're about to tell me what it is."

He tilts his head toward the night. "Did you hear something?"

"Don't change the subject by frightening me." I swallow. "You *were* just trying to change the subject, right?"

He gives me a mysterious look, which is completely ruined when his stomach rumbles so loudly it sounds like a train running through our lean-to. I realize I'm hungry, too.

"I brought snacks."

"By snacks do you mean a hamburger and French fries?"

I pull the pack onto my lap. "I had no idea you had a sense of humor," I say. "I had no idea you had a personality."

"I'm going to ignore that because you have food."

I rummage in my pack, a smile spreading through my veins. My fingers are stiff and the sweatshirt keeps slipping over my hand. I push up the sleeve. I really should give it back. Sam's got to be freezing, and besides, it's weird wearing his clothes. Personal. But I rub my cheek over the scratchy material bunched around my neck. Tomorrow will be here soon enough. Is it so wrong to want to wrap myself in tonight a little while longer?

My fingers dig into the main compartment and plastic wrappers crinkle. "Success," I say. I pull out a bag of trail mix and two granola bars. "A feast." I shine the light so I can read the labels on the bars. "Chocolate chip or peanut butter?"

He takes the chocolate chip and in less than a second the wrapper is gone and I hear him chewing. He moans softly.

I unwrap my own. It doesn't smell nearly as good. "Sweet tooth?"

"Quiet," he says around a mouthful. "I'm pretending this is a chocolate chip pancake."

My bar is dry and has that annoying taste of healthiness. "Why did you have to say that?"

"With syrup and butter. And bacon, extra crispy."

"Bacon," I say wistfully.

"You can share mine."

I bite off a hunk of granola but my imagination isn't as good as his. We're quiet while we finish our bars. I feel such a confusing mix of emotions. I'm sitting next to Sam, and the more time I spend with him, the less I feel like I know. This isn't the cold loner from class. It's also not the Sam from the funeral photo. That Sam was a boy, and this Sam is . . . not. I wanted to understand him, and it's ironic that it now feels as if he's the only one who can understand me.

The flashlight gleams across a puddle and turns the rainwater silver. It's one of the most beautiful things I've ever seen. I tear open the trail mix and hold out the bag. "Thank you," I say.

He stills. "For what?"

"For yesterday on the bus. For pulling me out of the rain. For putting me behind you when that bear was stalking us." I wait for him to say *I only did it for the money.*

He doesn't.

He says, "You're welcome."

He takes a handful of nuts and raisins and I do the same. We chew in companionable silence. Just beyond our lean-to, the ground is littered with muddy leaves and broken bits of tree and clumps of dirt. Already, I can see the hint of steam rising from the ground as the temperature shifts. Or maybe it's just the sadness rising inside me like a shroud. It'll be morning soon, and the feel of his shoulder will be a memory I won't be able to hold on to.

Cecily and I once had to make paper chains for our sixth-grade homeroom. She made one long strand that ended up stretching nearly across the whole room. I made a chain that branched out in seven different directions and then I connected more chains to those chains. It ended up looking like two spiders mating on the ceiling, but I liked all the interconnectedness.

Over the past few months, the strands of my life have been falling away like strips of paper. I told myself it didn't matter. A single chain worked just as well as a connected one. In fact, a single chain was clean and simple. I could do simple.

But now I know there's nothing simple about being alone.

I wad up the empty wrappers and store them in my pack. Outside, the sky is still a print of stars. I don't know why, but stars are one of the few things I never tried to photograph.

A weary sigh moves through him and then through me. His voice is low and tight as he says, "Why are you here, Grace? Really?"

I sigh, my eyes fluttering closed. "Ask me again in the morning."

"I'm asking now. You were looking for evidence in Phoenix. Everyone knew you were. Then suddenly you head up here on a bus. You found something, didn't you?"

39

July

There are three things in the envelope and they slide into my hand. One is a folded piece of white paper. There's also a clip of four hundred-dollar bills. The last is a thick blue booklet I recognize. Mom's passport. I'm not sure why it's in here—I thought she kept it in the safe, with mine. I double-check the envelope to be sure it's empty and then set it next to the backpack with my beautiful new camera.

I put the money in my back pocket and unfold the piece of paper. I shift it lengthwise so I can read the bits of type and rows of numbers. My mind feels like a sheet of frosted glass. Slick and opaque. I'm staring at the paper in front of me, but I see only odd shapes and blurred color. Blue and yellow. White. Zeros and ones. Bank records of some sort? There are curved lines at the top of the page—two that form the shape of an arrow. No, not an arrow. A plane.

My hands shake as I bring the paper closer to my eyes. It doesn't look like any airline ticket I've seen before, but that's what it is. An electronic ticket. As if those words are the key to a secret code, the letters and numbers begin to form into something almost recognizable.

FOP: CASH
ISSUE: 02FEB16
DATE: MAY 10
STAT: OPEN
CUST: AVA LARGO
NON ENDO

My eyes scan up again. May 10 departure. Two days after Mom's stroke. Two days after the FBI delivered the Target letter. Still, it doesn't make sense. Who is Ava Largo? Is she the one controlling this in some way? But how? And what is her plane ticket doing in Mom's closet?

I open the passport next, flipping it to the back page, to the picture of my mom. I close my eyes, open them again. I'm not seeing right. I can't be, because the woman in the picture is my mom. She's also a woman I've never seen before. Short dark hair. Black-rimmed glasses. Heavy blush on her cheeks. Purple lipstick.

And the name. Ava Largo.

The smooth glassy surface of my mind shatters.

Oh God.

The passport falls from my hands. I sink to the carpet of the house that will belong to the government in less than two weeks.

My mother is a thief.

I'm a thief.

Ava Largo.

And like a puzzle box, all the pieces suddenly click into place. She had an escape plan. An open plane ticket and a passport.

For one.

My prepaid phone rings. It's a number I've only given to one place: Hawthorne House.

When I answer, Terry's voice is high and frantic. "Grace, it's your mother. She's waking up."

40

August

I shut off the flashlight. I don't want Sam to see me. I want it to be so dark that I can distance myself from who I am.

"I never stopped believing in my mom," I tell Sam. "Not even after the indictment. I was sure there was someone else. Someone worse than her. You know? So that people would hear the story and say, 'What Janelle Pierce did was wrong, but we can understand why. We would have done the same thing.'" I'm shivering again, as if the wind is inside me.

"How could I believe the FBI—even for a minute? That would mean she'd purposely stolen from all those people and used me to do it. My own mother." Even now, the thought tears at me. "So I told myself she was doing it to protect me. That she was being bribed or threatened." I draw my knees up under the sweatshirt. "I sat by her side at the rehab center and I washed her hair and did her nails.

I massaged her atrophied muscles and I put cream on her dry skin. And the whole time, I told her she should have trusted me with the truth. That it was going to be okay because we were going to handle it together.

"Then on Wednesday . . ." I pause, backtracking. "You asked why I have the camera. It's because I found it on Wednesday afternoon. It was hidden inside a false electrical panel along with some documents and a few hundred dollars."

Relief brightens his expression. "You found the money?"

"Not the money. Not in the way you think. It was an escape plan. A false passport and an open plane ticket."

"A ticket to where?"

"One of the Cook Islands. I don't even know where that is."

He shifts so quickly some of the branches are knocked loose. The sky is clear above the limbs of the pine tree. I think of how Mom described this place. *Trees as tall as forever.* She could have read that in a trail guide.

"Don't you get it, Grace? If she planned a new life for you, she would have needed money."

"You didn't let me finish." My shoulders are shaking now. "I found *one* airline ticket. *One* passport. She wasn't planning a new life for the two of us. She was leaving and she didn't care what happened to me."

"What?"

"One t-t-ticket. One."

"Jesus, Grace. You're shivering."

"I'm f-fine."

"All right. Okay." His words are a low murmur, and I think he's worried I'm going to shatter into a million pieces. "Hang on."

He's out of the shelter before I register that he's moved. There's rustling overhead, and suddenly the sky is a canvas of stars. My jacket snaps like a bit of parachute being shaken out, and then he ducks back inside and sets my coat over my knees.

"I know it's wet, but it'll keep the wind off."

"Don't," I say. "Don't be nice to me."

"Just listen. Okay?" He sits down beside me, our shoulders nearly touching. "You have no idea what she was thinking. She probably figured you were too young to be accused."

"She knew," I say. "She knew exactly what would happen. What people would think. What my life would be like. She didn't love me. She never loved me."

"Grace." He touches my arm and I jerk away.

"No." I never want anyone to touch me again.

"Maybe she planned to get herself settled and then send for you."

"You don't think I've considered that?" My voice is thick with bitterness. "I've thought of all sorts of explanations, because that's what I've been really good at all these months. But here's the other possibility: My mom used me. From the very beginning. Every brochure photo I smiled for. Every event I attended. Every time she told me how the business was for my benefit, how I was the most important person in her life. She lied to me. Every single thing she said was a lie."

"Grace, don't."

"What's it say about me that my own mother couldn't love me? What kind of person am I?"

He shifts to my side and puts an arm around my shoulders.

"No!"

"Just until you're warm." Both of his arms are around me now and I push him away, raising my arms like a barrier between us. He smells of sweat and mud and I can't breathe against his stiff shirt. "I told you not to be nice to me."

"I'm trying my best," he says. "You're not making it easy." His heart beats under my cheek, steady and strong. Somehow, my arms are around his back and he pulls me closer. One hand soothes the muscles between my shoulder blades and the other one cups the back of my head. His fingers slide into my awful hair and I give in to the kindness of his touch.

"Tell me why you're here?" he asks.

"I don't want to. You'll hate me more than you already do."

"I don't hate you, Grace." His breath whispers over my forehead. "I want to, but that's not the same thing."

I shake my head and he holds me tighter, murmuring, "It's okay."

When I tell him the truth, he'll pull away, but I can't put it off any longer. And so I describe a little girl and her mother and a story about a picture buried up on a mountain in southern Colorado. I whisper the words to his shirt and I pray that the heart beneath is big enough to hold them. "And that's why I'm here," I finish.

He stiffens. "Because of a picture in a jar?"

I can't blame him for sounding incredulous. Angry. I ease back, but there's nowhere to escape. I dip my head; I feel so exposed. I've let the barriers between us fall and I wish I could gather them again, use them to shield me from his disappointment. "That's why I didn't say anything. Because it sounds ridiculous even to my own ears. People have lost their futures and I'm up here looking for a picture."

He's quiet for a long time. Above the horizon, shades of gray are slowly emerging from the black. Daylight is on its way.

"But it's not the picture, is it?" he finally asks.

"No," I say.

"You want to know if she told you the truth."

My throat is too full to answer.

"Because if she did . . . if the picture is up here . . ."

"Then maybe she loved me after all." Tears blind me as I admit to Sam what I've been afraid to admit to myself. "It shouldn't matter. I know that. She's a monster. My mother is a monster. But I still need to know if she loved me. If she ever loved me."

He looks out into the shifting sky. "If I thought Marcus had left me something . . ." His voice shakes. "If there was the smallest chance, I'd climb to the moon to find it." He sighs and then says matter-of-factly, "So. We're here to find a glass jar."

I'm not sure what he says after that. I'm crying too hard to hear.

41

August

The birds are twittering. Long, bright snippets of sound that slip under my eyelids. When I open my eyes, weak light streams in from above while grays and golds shimmer on the wet trees. I must have nodded off again.

Sunrise. A new day.

Saturday.

Along with the light comes memory. Reality. Tomorrow is Sunday, and whatever life my mother has left will be over. The decision to live or die has already been made for her. I think of the pills still folded inside my blue bandana.

What decision will I make for myself? Can I live with what I find?

Slowly I unwind from my ball of sleep and push myself upright with one arm. Muscles I didn't know I have cramp tightly and I groan with the pain. Everything hurts. My butt. My feet. My torn hands. My swollen eyes.

The spot beside me is empty, and when I peek out of the shelter, the air still feels heavy with unshed rain. I don't see Sam, though his pack is here. Standing gingerly, I breathe in the clammy, cool air and the smell of earth and pine trees. Birds flap above, and I catch a glimpse of movement as the twittering stops and then starts again. I wonder if birds mean the bear is gone.

My stomach is empty but I'm not hungry. Once I find the trail, it will only be four or five hours to where I need to go.

I find a tree for privacy, not walking far because my legs refuse to work properly. Just how high did we scramble up that mountain? When I'm done, I hobble my way toward the valley, searching for a broader view. Is Sam hunting for a way down? Or did he just need to get away? Everything will look different to him in the light of day. I used to think that was a good thing.

I wonder what color the trees will be when the sunrise reaches the top? Yellow? Gold? Amber, like the color of Sam's eyes? I can still feel the shape of him next to me, the warmth of him. But it's a little like the mist clinging to the hills. The sun will rise and then the mist will be gone, burned off by reality.

I'm still Grace Pierce, daughter of Janelle Pierce. I am part of the worst financial scam in the state of Arizona. I am the face of ruin and betrayal. No matter where I go or what I do, that is always who I'll be. And the one person who could have helped me survive this is the one person who betrayed me.

"Hey."

Sam's voice comes from just behind me and I startle, my hand flying to my chest. "I didn't hear you."

When I turn, I have to smile. He's a rumpled mess. Dirt is smudged across his crooked nose and caked down his neck. His hair is littered with dust and leaves. Beneath my ribs, I feel an ache. I want to pick the leaves free. I want to hold his hand and stop the restless scratching of his arm. I want to take pictures of him catching lizards in the desert and laughing while he does it. Something about Sam has always pulled at me, ever since I saw that picture. What I saw then, and didn't understand, was his loneliness. Now I do. Now I feel it myself as if our hurts are two halves of the same whole. I wanted to heal Sam and now I have no idea how to heal either one of us.

I turn toward the horizon, watching droplets of water turn to diamonds on the leaves. I hold up my hands, touching my thumbs and raising my pointer fingers to create a window. "Did you ever do this?" I ask.

"Make a finger frame?" He nods. "Yeah."

"I used to do it all the time. We'd be driving somewhere or Cecily and I would be at the mall. Sometimes I'd look around the lunchroom at school and capture it all with my finger frame." I shift the frame over the expanse of mountains and sky. "I never realized until now, but so much of photography for me was sharing the pictures." My fingers drop.

Twigs snap as he shifts beside me. "I knew something must have happened on Wednesday."

Wednesday. The day I found the cubby. The day the hospital called to say Mom was waking up. "How?"

He slides his hands into his pockets. "There's a spot on the ridgeline a couple blocks from your house. I go there sometimes because I can see your house from up top. I saw the cab."

"Did you follow me?"

"I couldn't. Not from up there."

"Bad detective work, Mr. Rivers."

"I followed you here, didn't I?"

"Yeah. And it just about got you killed by lightning."

"Don't forget about the bear."

I smile, but it fades after only a second. Memory pulls me back to that day. "I'd already found the hidden cubby—I'm not sure how long I was lying on the closet floor. But the phone rang, and when I heard Terry's voice, I ran for my car keys. I forgot I didn't have a car. All I could think about was that my mom was waking up. That's what Terry told me."

"But she never did?"

I shake my head. "She opened her eyes. She might even have been conscious for a few minutes. But by the time I got to Hawthorne House, she was in an ambulance on her way back to the hospital. She'd had a second stroke. A major event, they called it. It made me think of the Academy Awards—a major event. When really, it was a brain bleed.

"I had to take another cab," I continue. "But I didn't have enough money for the fare. I gave the cabbie my ring.

It was a Celtic knot Mom had given me." I hold up my pinkie. There's still a strip of white from where I tanned around it. "I'd turned the ring into this symbol of unending love—I thought that's what it meant. But then I looked it up and a Celtic knot means eternity. She probably thought it was pretty. She probably didn't even know what it was."

"You don't know that."

"Exactly," I say. "That's the point. I don't know anything. All these months I've been waiting for her to wake up and then they called and I thought *Finally!* But she never spoke. She never said a single word." I shudder. "I think about that a lot. One word. If she could have just said one word. You know?"

"Yeah." He wipes his hands over his face. "Marcus never woke up, either. The doctors said the damage was too extensive, but I was still so sure he'd open his eyes. Marcus could always do things no one expected."

"How long was he in a coma?"

"Two days."

"Do you think . . ." I pause. Swallow. "Do you think he was there? That he knew you were there?"

"I hope not."

Surprised, I glance up at him. "Why?"

"Because I told him to go ahead and die if that's what he wanted." His voice chokes on the last word. He turns away. I want to touch his arm, the curve of his back. But even as I think it, he straightens, pulling into himself. He's so much stronger than I am. Strong the way I need to be if

I'm going to survive this. When he turns back, his eyes are shuttered again.

"I've been thinking," he says.

My heart drops. I already know what he's going to say.

"Your mother obviously made plans. Plans that required money. She had a false identity."

"Sam." I sigh. "Before I caught the bus, I told the FBI. They already knew about Ava Largo. They still haven't turned up any offshore accounts."

"You gave them the plane information?"

"I sent them copies of everything."

"So something could turn up on that island." He runs a hand through his hair, his gaze sweeping over the treetops. "What if the proof is somewhere else?"

"It's not up here, Sam. Even if the money does exist, it couldn't be."

"Why not?"

"Because that jar with a picture in it was a silly story told to a little girl who wanted to go on a trip with her mom. It's been two years since we even talked about it. Two years since she claimed to have been here."

"What do you mean 'claimed'?"

"I don't think she was ever here at all. I tried to track down her hiking partner and discovered there wasn't one. I went back over old Visa statements and couldn't find any travel records."

"Doesn't mean there aren't any. Or maybe she paid cash."

"What about the plane ticket? The departure was scheduled two days after the FBI delivered that letter. She had to know about the investigation. If there was money, why not give herself more time to climb a mountain before she caught a plane?"

"Unless she was going to get word to you once she was out of the country. And you were going to climb the mountain."

"That's wishful thinking."

He steps closer, his eyes intense. "No. It's crazy thinking. And you know what Mr. Dean says. There's a fine line between crazy and creative."

I shake my head, but my pulse quickens.

"She must have guessed the FBI would go through the house. That they might find the hidden panel. She wouldn't have wanted to put everything in one place. Save herself some secrets, right?"

I hate what I hear in his voice. The energy. The hum of excitement.

"Where is the picture hidden, exactly?"

"There are three lakes. Lower Blue Lake, a middle lake about a quarter mile above that, and then Upper Blue Lake. There's a cliff that looks over the middle lake. A place where you'll feel like you're on top of the world."

"And then?"

"There's a cairn—a stack of boulders as tall as a person. She put the jar inside, where it would be protected from the weather."

"Did she write that down anywhere? Tell anyone besides you?"

"I don't know. I don't think so."

He turns to face the mountain. The highest peak, and whatever secrets it holds, is hidden in the clouds. "Maybe that bottle has what we both need."

I let myself imagine it, see what he sees. If the money is there, I could give Sam back his future. Maybe I could give us both back our futures.

"Sam," I say. "Don't get your hopes up."

But I feel my own rising.

42

August

At first there isn't a trail. We have to make our own, testing for the best way through the ridge of trees. A blister on my little toe and another on my heel announce themselves with every step. My socks are still damp, which doesn't help, and neither does the mud that sucks at my shoes. I'm wearing my jacket again, and Sam has his sweatshirt back. We're both layered in grime. I don't think I've ever been this filthy before.

Sam keeps turning to check on me, and I hate the way it makes me feel. Like he cares. Like we're friends. Which is why I snap, "Stop it!" after he does it for the fifth time.

He pauses to face me. "Stop what?"

"Stop checking on me."

"It's steep. I'm worried you'll fall."

"I know what you're worried about."

He rolls his eyes, but he doesn't look back again. That makes me even angrier. At myself.

As we continue, the undergrowth gets thicker and the boulders grow larger. I struggle over them, my heart thumping against my sternum as drop-offs appear to my right. Sam doesn't seem to be scared of anything, and it reassures me. So when he skids sharply down a muddy slope, I'm the one who cries out.

"I'm okay," he calls.

Then he reappears, even muddier but smiling. He grips a tree with one hand and plants his foot on a web of roots to brace himself. He leans forward and stretches a hand toward me. I let go of my pride and clutch him, my palm on his wrist, his on mine, until I'm safely down.

After that, we stay close as we move forward. Our labored breaths are punctuated with short bursts of words.

This way.

Careful. This branch has thorns.

Icy patch over here.

The trees are thick in places, the shrubs sharp and grasping. I'm ducking under one, careful after the last one scraped my forearm, and I nearly bump into him. "What?"

He points to a pile of poop.

My pulse skips. "Bear?" I ask.

He looks around, and from the way he tugs at the neck of his sweatshirt, I wonder if he has the same creeping sensation I do. Like we're being watched. "Or something worse," he says.

We freeze, both of us straining to hear, but there's nothing. Almost an eerie nothing. A bear would make noise. A bear would come crashing through the trees.

Or something worse.

The things I read on the Internet filter through my mind. Birds. Bears. *Mountain lions.*

"Come on," he says.

Moving more quickly, Sam jogs through a muddy patch and I follow as closely as I can, my heart urging me to go even faster. Abruptly, we come out of the trees and the valley stretches out below and around us. The sun is like a scoop of vanilla ice cream over the mountain. The warmth of the rays feels good enough for me to want to roll my wet self in sunshine and bake.

I look back the way we came, but I can't see anything. The weird feeling is gone, too.

"Look," he says, pointing just below us. "There's the trail."

"Now we just have to hope Mr. Bear isn't waiting for us."

"Mr. Bear?"

"I'm being respectful."

He starts toward the trail and I fall in behind him. "If you do get eaten, can I have your camera? I know it's some big dark secret. Your camera, your technique . . ."

"It's not a secret."

"Then show me."

"Nope."

I stomp my way over an uneven patch of boulders. "I may be earnest, but you're brooding."

He says nothing, but he's smiling again. Why does he have to have such a perfect smile?

Once we're safely on the trail, it's easier to cover ground, and it isn't long before I recognize the field of wildflowers from the day before. It's seven-thirty when I check my watch. We should be back at the main trail soon, and then we'll have about four miles to the upper lake.

Will the cairn be there?

Will it be like she said?

I hear the rumble of a car from the parking lot first, and a few minutes later the breeze carries the sound of voices. *Finally, the trail junction!* There's a group of hikers gathered, and I could hug every one of them. When a dog begins barking at us, I think I could hug it, too. After that bear, I'll never be afraid of a dog again. It's a cute little guy, actually. Shaggy brown fur and floppy ears. It jumps up, straining as we get closer. A little girl has hold of the leash and she cries out when the handle is yanked from her grip.

The dog rushes toward us, the leash flapping behind. Sam is quicker—stepping in front of me and grabbing the dog's scruff before it can reach me. "Settle," he says, while the puppy yips and jumps.

"I'm so sorry," a woman says, running up. She's breathless as she takes the leash and folds the squirming dog in her arms. "That's enough, Max."

Behind her the girl runs up. She's a skinny thing in a red

hat with a canteen around her neck. Her breath is coming hard. "I'm sorry. I'm really sorry."

"It's my fault," the woman says. "I shouldn't have given her the leash. Max is friendly, but he's also a puppy without any manners."

"I didn't see them coming," the girl says to her mom, her voice wobbly with tears. "I would have held him harder, but I didn't see."

"I know," she says. "It's okay, honey." She reaches out a hand and her daughter takes it. I watch their fingers twine and clasp. See the way they fit together so sweetly.

"Excuse me," I say abruptly. "I need more water." My bottle is still half full, but I have to get away before I splinter yet again.

Sam follows me to the parking lot, crouching by me at the spigot.

"Grace? You okay?"

"Fine." I finish with my bottle and move back to the trail. Sam curses behind me, stalled at the spigot while he refills his. I move fast, blinking hard to keep my vision clear. I'm barely back on the trail when I hear his heavy footsteps behind me.

"Wait!"

"I'm fine."

I pass the logbook and two women with hiking poles. I'm skirting another fallen limb when Sam jumps it and cuts me off.

"Would you stop for a minute?" I try to get around

him, but he moves faster than me. "Look, I'm sorry about
the dog. I tried to catch it before it could rush you."

"You did."

"Then . . ."

"It's not the dog."

"Jesus, Grace. Would you stop?"

I sigh and rub my face. "It's the mother and her daughter," I say. "I used to squeeze my mom's hand the exact
same way. I used to . . ."

He takes my hand and pulls me off the trail. A young
couple, bent under the weight of their heavy green packs,
waves as they pass.

"Tell me," he says.

"It's just a memory."

"Of your mom?"

"It was stupid."

"Tell me," he says again.

"I got in trouble when I was in the second grade. I sat
in black paint and a girl named Abigail told everyone in
the class that I'd had an accident in my underwear. I shook
my fist at her and the teacher sent me to the principal for
violent behavior."

"Violent?"

"They had to be very careful in case the other girl told
her mom she was threatened and no action had been taken.
So I went to the office and the principal called my mother.
She swept in smelling of gardens, looking beautiful in
her black dress and her hair in a French knot. She made

everyone else look shabby—that was how it always was. I wanted her to be proud of me, you know? I felt awful that she'd had to leave work—that I'd disappointed her." I draw in a long breath. "I was ridiculously easy to punish—the silent treatment was enough to make me crumble. But when we got in the car, she turned to face me and said, 'Show me.' I had no idea what she meant. 'Show me your fist,' she said.

"When I did, she moved my thumb from under my fingers and said, 'Try it that way or you'll break your own bones.' It was as if she wasn't even mad. I couldn't believe it. I kept saying how sorry I was that she had to come for me. 'Don't be ridiculous,' she told me in her impatient voice. 'I'll always come for you.'"

Brushing away tears, I laugh at my own reaction. "It's such a good memory. I don't know why it makes me cry."

"Because the bad memories are bad," Sam says. "But the good memories are worse."

I forget he understands things I'm only beginning to.

"I can't make sense of it. You know?"

He yanks at the tall stem of a flower. I've seen a few of them along the trail, the white petals looking as soft as silk, the scent reminding me of Mom's perfume. The stem comes free. "It isn't supposed to be this way. The people who betray us should be strangers. Enemies. Not the people who are supposed to love us. But that's what makes it betrayal. Because we trusted them. Because we let them in where they could do the most damage."

With one quick brush of his fingers, the petals fall. All that's left is the stem. He tosses it back into the brush.

"So what do you do?" I ask.

His eyes are a closed lens. I wonder, if I could adjust the aperture—could pour light in through his pupil—what would I see? He sighs. "You don't let anyone get close."

43

August

"We must be nearly there."

I stop and look at the mountain. I don't actually think we're close at all, but I need an excuse to rest. We've been hiking for forty minutes and the air is pretty much non-existent. The Internet called the trail strenuous. That must be hiker's code for *Prepare not to breathe.* It's not even a trail. It's more like a never-ending ramp that goes straight up. The lake is beginning to feel like a mirage, only you're supposed to be able to see mirages and I see almost nothing but the two-by-two patch of dirt under my feet as I take each step.

A woman with white hair and sagging skin passes us coming down. She's running—she calls hello as we step aside. I watch her, shocked that she can move that fast and still form intelligible words. I'm practically wheezing. "You think she ran all the way up?"

"No," Sam says. "She had a wristband on. She took the elevator."

I expend energy I don't have to glare at Sam. "That's not even funny."

"It's the altitude. You're not used to it."

"*You're* doing fine."

"I run eight miles a day."

He looks it, too. Ridiculously fit, even though he's hiking a mountain in jeans and shoes that must weigh ten pounds. "Why couldn't I have had an out-of-shape stalker?"

He sighs dramatically. "Life is full of disappointments."

I want to stick out my tongue, but even more I want to smile. I like this Sam. His dry sense of humor. His gruff kindness. The tiny bow that curves above his top lip when he's not scowling.

He reties the lace on one shoe. "It's still early. Sit for a few if you need to."

"I won't be able to get up. Ow!" I glance down at my arm where something has just stung me. Some *things*. There are four raised bumps turning red beneath the layer of dirt on my arm, and yet another scrape I don't remember getting.

He steps closer, dipping his head to see. "You're bleeding."

"It's nothing. It doesn't hurt half as bad as everything else. My legs feel like the pulp of a cantaloupe. My heels feel like raw hamburger."

"Someone is hungry."

"From that you got food?"

He smiles. "Maybe I'm the one who's hungry. You should clean that."

"With what? Everything I have is just as dirty as my arm."

"There's a bandana in your pack."

Before I can stop him, he's got my backpack off and in his arms. The zipper sounds even as I cry out, "Wait—no!"

Then he has the scrap of material and he's shaking it loose. Pills sprinkle out, a shower of white and baby blue.

Sam goes still. The air begins to vibrate with tension. "What are those?"

I drop to my knees and pick up one pill and then another. I reach for a third, but Sam steps on it, driving it into the wet earth.

"It's medicine."

"Bullshit. What are they?" He squats down, gathering up more of the pills before I can. He shakes them in the palm of his hand.

"Sleeping pills. I have nightmares. You've seen that for yourself."

"These aren't sleeping pills. Valium?" He reads the word on one pill and then flips over the white one. "Xanax?" His eyes bore into me. "You need a handful of both for a day hike? What the hell is going on?"

"Nothing. Okay? Nothing." My voice rises as if I can push him away with sheer volume.

He doesn't budge. He suddenly looks like he's made of the same granite as these mountains. "You're planning to kill yourself? Where? Up at the top? Were you going to mention that or was I supposed to watch and hand you the water bottle while you downed them?"

"You weren't supposed to be here!"

"Are you fucking kidding me?" In his crouched position, I'm reminded of a lion before it strikes. His jaw is clenched, his voice an angry growl.

"There's not going to be anything up there, Sam."

"And this was your Plan B? Pills?"

"We flew on private jets," I say. "My mother bought a hundred-thousand-dollar rug because she was bored by the old one. I had flip-flops that cost a thousand dollars. I—"

"Shut up!" he roars. He shoots to his feet and I do the same. But I've been quiet for too long.

"People's lives were destroyed because of my mother. Because of me."

"So you fix it," he says.

"You don't think I've tried? It can't be fixed."

"Everything can be fixed with money."

"*If* the money exists, and that's a very big if. With the pills . . . at least everyone gets their pound of flesh."

"Damn it, Grace!" His face is pale. "You don't get off that easy." He squeezes the pills in his hand and then throws them hard down the slope of the mountain.

"No!" I cry, my arm shooting out uselessly. But they're gone.

"You stay and you deal," Sam says. "You don't get to check out."

"Oh yeah?" My eyes burn as I look at him. "And who says? You? You've checked out. You come to school every day, but you're like negative space in a photo. You're what isn't there."

"You don't know a thing—"

"You're right!" I interrupt. "I don't know what your story is. If it's grief or it's drugs—you're always in long-sleeve shirts scratching like you're late for your next fix. But maybe that's the trick. Maybe you pull away however you can. So I've been trying to act the same way. Cold and cut off. And you know what? I don't want to be like you." My voice cracks, drenching my words in sobs. "I don't want to be alone. I don't want to hate everyone and have everyone hate me."

I stumble back a few steps. I'm scraped up and bleeding from places deep inside of me that I know will never heal. "I don't want to live like this. I won't, you understand? I won't!"

I turn and run for the trail. I push off a fallen log and wince as I hit the packed dirt. My left knee explodes with pain.

But it isn't me who screams.

It's Sam.

44

August

When I turn, Sam is crumpled over the log I just crossed.

It takes me a second to make sense of what I see. There's frayed bark and chips of wood scattered over the trail. Rotting moss and mud spills like guts from a hollow in the log that wasn't there minutes ago. And Sam's leg is buried nearly up to the knee. The log must be rotten. It held my weight but collapsed under Sam's, trapping him. Even as I watch, he tries to free himself. The sound of his jeans tearing makes me wince.

Run.

The voice in my head isn't a whisper. It's a shout.

Blood races through my veins, urging me to go. *It'll be easier if I'm alone, if it's only my dreams shattered and not his.*

Above me the trail is straight for a few more yards and then dips to the right. Ten steps, maybe twelve, and I can disappear around that corner.

I hesitate.

Sam tugs at his leg again and slowly works it free. My breath catches. He's already fine—he'll be after me in another few seconds.

Then he sets his foot on even ground, and it twists. Buckles. His face knots with pain and he sinks over the decayed log. His head lifts, and when our gazes meet, he nods—as if he knows. As if he's saying it's okay. He would go if our places were reversed.

I take a step. *He'll be fine. He's strong. Even if he is hurt, someone will come along. Someone will make sure he gets back down.*

I shuffle another step. Then another.

And I end up by Sam's side.

He's hunched over, weight on his left leg, his face pale and his jaw clenched.

"Come on," I say. "Let's get you off that leg."

He blinks up at me. I don't know if it's a trick of the light, of the sun finding a way through the trees to spark the gold of his eyes. I don't know if I'm only seeing what I want to see. But it feels so real my heart presses against my rib cage. The wariness is gone. His beautiful, tired eyes meet mine, hiding nothing. They're the eyes of a boy who is just as lost and bewildered as I am. The eyes of the boy I half fell in love with from just one picture.

"Don't take those pills, Grace."

"Come on," I say softly. "Let's get you up."

"Grace."

I can't ignore the plea in his voice. "Most of them are halfway down the mountain." I position myself under his arm so I can take some of his weight.

"You know what I mean."

"I know." He rests one hand on my right shoulder and I ready myself, tightening my core and bracing my legs. I slide my hand around his waist. "It's the guilt," I say softly. "It gets to be too much sometimes. I just needed to feel like I had a choice."

"That's not a choice," he says. "That's the end of every choice."

Though I never met his dead brother, I can feel him between us. Beside us. I wonder if Sam carries him everywhere. If I'll carry my mom with me the same way. "Let's head for that boulder." I gesture with my head to a relatively large and flat rock a short ways off the trail. Still I can feel him holding back. "It's okay, Sam. I've got you."

For a long moment, it doesn't seem as if he's even breathing. Then his weight shifts. When he leans on me, I feel a shift within myself. My eyes sting and I understand all of a sudden that what I was really asking for—and what he just granted me—was his trust.

We shuffle together toward the boulder. He's heavier than I expect, and I press even closer. So close I can hear the beat of his heart against my temple. My breath adjusts to its rhythm, and despite everything, I feel a sense of calm.

It only takes a few minutes to work through the brush and pines to the boulder. He hops the final few steps, using one hand to brace his weight as he sits on the nearly flat surface. Wincing, he stretches out his right leg and tugs up the hem of his jeans.

The skin of his calf has been scraped raw. Blood bubbles up, and when I touch the top of his black sock it's damp. I don't think it's sweat. But the ankle itself is going to be the problem. It's already swelling and turning a reddish purple. I think that means blood under the skin. "Can you take off your shoe?"

"It's probably better if I don't. I might not get it back on."

His shoe has a heavy bottom with a thick tread and stiff sides that tie an inch or two higher than tennis shoes. I'm not sure if that's good or bad. "I don't know what to do. Elevate it, I think." I pull off my pack and set it on the boulder. He raises his leg and sets it on my makeshift pillow, his mouth tightening with the effort.

"Is it broken?"

He shakes his head. "Torn ligaments, maybe. I've sprained it before."

"I had a broken finger once," I say helpfully. "My mom splinted it. RICE," I add, pulling the acronym from some place deep in my brain where I'm also storing every line of dialogue from The Lion King and the original Pokémon theme song. "Rest. Ice." I frown. "The last one is elevation." I start again, hoping it'll come to me if I say it quickly enough. "Rest. Ice. Cereal."

"Compression," Sam says with a crooked smile.

I want to photograph that smile. I want to photograph his every smile. Embarrassed at my own thoughts, I refocus on his ankle. "Right! Compression. Which is good, because we have no cereal. Should I try to wrap it?"

He shakes his head. "Maybe just tighten the laces."

Nodding, I move to the end of the boulder and lean over the toe, but that seems awkward. I end up beside him, one knee resting on the rock while I work to loosen the knots. My fingers are stiff and the laces are leather and stuck. Not a good combination.

"You couldn't wear tennis shoes like everyone else?"

"I did," he says, "until I was taking photos at a construction site and got a nail in the side of my foot."

The laces finally come loose. I straighten the tongue and smooth the top edges of his shoe. "Was that when you got the shot of the metal beams?"

"Yeah." The word is a croak as I begin pulling the laces as tight as I can.

"Did you set that shot up?" I ask.

He shakes his head, his eyes squeezed closed.

The shot was of two steel beams, old and corroding, part of the fallen building being cleared away to make room for new money coming into the downtown area. The beams had fallen to look exactly like a cross. The class argued whether the image was one of belief . . . or the end of belief.

"What was the point you were trying to make?" I ask.

He opens one eye in a squint. "What do you think?"

I finish with the lace, wincing myself as I make it as tight as I can against the ballooning ankle. "I think I hate when people answer questions with questions." I pull out the bandana without disturbing his foot and use his water bottle to soak the material. Wrinkling my nose at his torn skin, I do my best to blot the blood and clean away the dirt. "I think it's a choice. To believe or not believe. I used to think it was easier to believe."

"And now?"

I wrap the bandana around the worst of the scrape and tie it in place. "I think it's safer not to." I sit back and admire my work. "That should hold until you get down."

"I'm not going down."

"Of course you're going down."

He tests the tightness of my bandage. "I'm climbing this mountain." Then his head dips and he adds in a low grumble, "And I don't hate everyone."

My cheeks burn with a flush. "Oh."

"I'm not on drugs. I don't cut myself." His hand rises to his right forearm, a movement so practiced it seems like it's a part of him. "What I am," he says, "is screwed up."

His gaze locks with mine. Slowly, he pulls up his sleeve.

45

August

His skin is pale, but healthy muscle ripples from his forearm to his elbow as he pushes the material higher. I'm
holding my breath as I see the curve of his bicep and the
deep line of his triceps.

A line that's striped with a bright red rash.

"I started scratching after Marcus died," he says. "I didn't
even know I was doing it at first. I'd wake up like a cat running its claws down a post. The doctor prescribed a cream.
It doesn't help."

I raise my fingers to his arm, shocked at myself when I
touch the raised red bumps. "Sorry." I pull away, my face as
hot as his skin.

"It's okay." He tugs down his sleeve.

"Does it hurt?"

"Not really."

I ease back onto the boulder beside him. "Why do you
hide it?"

"I'd rather everyone thought it was drugs."

"But it's not your fault that Marcus died. It was an accident."

"That's not what you asked earlier."

My own words sting as he repeats them now. "Did Marcus play with death? Did I help him?"

I scrape my thumb over a ridge in the boulder. "It's what I heard. What kids said at school. I didn't know what to believe."

He swings his legs off the boulder and pushes his pant leg down. "Kids had a lot to say after it happened. Most of it bullshit, but the part about death was true. Marcus was playing a game of asphyxiation."

My thumb snags on a sharp point. I hardly feel the pain. "A what?"

"Yeah, it's real fun." He's shifted sideways, showing me only his profile. A muscle twitches in his cheek. "You and your buddies get together and you choke each other."

"I . . . I don't understand."

His voice is flat, disconnected from the words he's saying. "It takes three people. One guy stands still while another puts him in a choke hold. A few seconds later, the air is gone and the person passes out. But first their diaphragm starts to spasm and their arms flail."

"My God," I whisper. "That's a game?"

"Because when you pass out, you get a rush." The tips of his fingers turn white against the boulder. "That's what these idiots were after—a rush. Never mind that it can fry your brain or end up killing you."

"What's the third guy do?"

"He videotapes it."

I feel as faint as if there were hands around my own neck.

Sam slides forward, testing his hurt leg on the uneven ground. "Marcus showed me the videos on YouTube. I didn't get it—at all. Told him it was the dumbest thing I'd ever seen. That was before he started flying solo. His words," he adds, flashing me a quick look of disgust. "I caught him at it about a month before he died. He was using a belt to choke himself." He rubs a hand over his eyes. "We had one hell of a fight. I said he had shit for brains. He said I wouldn't understand because I had it too easy. Because I didn't know what it was like carrying all that responsibility around like a pair of shoulder pads you never take off. He said right before everything goes dark the worries just float away. You float away. Free."

His hand is scratching his arm again. I lean across the boulder and cover his fingers with mine. "Don't." I can't stand to watch him shredding his skin, knowing that must be the way he feels inside.

He pushes himself up, limping a few feet until he's standing in a raw shaft of sunlight. "I didn't know he was so trapped. I didn't know it was so bad for him. That I was such a drain my brother had to check out permanently."

"Sam." I come around the boulder. "He wasn't trying to die."

His eyes meet mine. His irises are dark with pain. "What

if he was? Because he did take care of me. He took care of the three of us."

"You were just a kid."

"So was he. My dad took off when I was eight. Waved to us from the open window of the truck and told us we could come see him whenever we wanted. Marcus said we weren't ever going to see that asshole. He said we'd be fine and we were. He just . . . stepped in." Sam's gaze lifts into the distance . . . into his past. "Did everything while he kept up his grades and made every football highlight reel in the country. He's the one who took care of things while Mom worked. I'd wake up in the morning, and Marcus would be making lunches in the kitchen. I'd sit at the table with my Game Boy and he'd pour milk in my cereal. I can hear the sound of it—the splash of the milk, the crackle of the cereal flakes. My thumbs clacking over the controls." He hunches over his leg, rubbing his ankle, and I wonder if it hurts or if it's the only pain he knows how to reach.

"It was an accident," I say. "A stupid, stupid accident."

"I should've stopped him."

"You tried."

"I mean that night. I was there that night." He leans a hand against a tree, then suddenly makes a fist and punches the trunk.

"Sam!"

"Goddamn him!" he shouts.

"Sam," I say again. I take his hand, brushing splinters

from his skin, smoothing fingers over his torn knuckles. Wishing I could do so much more.

"He was two weeks from graduation. He had a full ride to Alabama." He stares at his hand as if he doesn't recognize it. "We had it all planned out. He was going to leave in June and I was going to spend the summer with him. But that night . . ."

Sam tugs his hand free, pressing his thumb against the scrapes as if he needs it to hurt more. "Mom called for me to come down for dinner. Asked me to knock on Marcus's door in case he was sleeping. It was the same as every other night. Mom likes to cook us dinner. She's got a good business cleaning office buildings, but the hours suck. She gets home around three a.m. and then sleeps in until we're gone for school. So dinner is the only time we're together." He shifts his weight, so he can lean his back against the tree. "But I was playing a video game online with my buddy Jerrod. I was pissed that I was going to lose if my mom didn't stop distracting me. So I yelled for her to give me a minute." He releases a long breath. "It was more than a minute. More than a few minutes. And Marcus wasn't napping on the other side of my bedroom wall."

Hesitantly, I step closer. "You didn't know. You couldn't have known."

His head is so low his chin nearly touches his chest. "I'm the one who found him. At least there was that. I got him free of the belt before I screamed for Mom. He wouldn't have wanted her to see that. We called nine-one-one but it was too late."

When he looks up, his eyes glimmer like wet leaves. "I would have done more, but how the hell did I know what he was thinking? Was I supposed to be a mind reader? He was Marcus Rivers. He handled everything."

He sighs and straightens, steadying himself on both feet. "I swore to my mom that I was going to take care of things. That it was going to be okay. We didn't need Marcus. We just needed money so I could get us set up in New Jersey near my aunt. Mom was going to open the same kind of business and I was going to study photography in New York."

"Oh God," I breathe. "The Family Fund."

He nods, his gaze locked to mine. "The money has to be here. We have to find it."

He limps to where the trees are thickest and crouches down. His fingers sift through the dirt like flour, flinging sticks and leaves.

"What are you doing?"

He comes up with a long broken branch and hefts it in his hands. Standing, he jabs it at the ground, testing the strength. It's just tall enough to serve as a walking stick.

"You can't hike up the mountain."

"I can if you help me." He braces his weight on the stick and walks back to me.

The knuckles of his hurt hand turn white—with pain or determination I don't know. His eyes plead with me, his mask gone. "You have to help me, Grace. I can't fuck up one more thing."

46

August

The trail has turned muddy, and it's slow going with Sam's ankle. We take turns leading, but I'm not doing much better than he is. My knee aches from coming down hard on the trail, but it's hardly noticeable next to the throbbing of my blisters. I bite my lip against the worst of it, but each time a pained gasp slips out, Sam stops, pretending he needs to check his ankle to give me a rest.

The third time I'm torn between wanting to cry and wanting to smile. I go with crying. Not much—just a few weak tears of exhaustion.

"Your feet?" he asks.

I shake my head. "You. You're just so nice. You're so . . ." I sigh at my own hesitation. He probably won't be talking to me soon. Why not say it now? "I'm really glad you're here."

"Now I know you're delirious."

"I'll always—"

His eyes widen and he holds a finger to his lips. "Did you hear that?"

Voices.

He points to my right and through the trees I see a flash of green that is way too neon to be natural. "What is that?"

"Looks like a tent. Is there a campsite up here?"

"By the lower lake."

His face softens with a grin. "Come on." He takes my hand and we limp together past a string of colorful tents and an arrow sign pointing ahead to Lower Blue Lake. The trees suddenly drop away and the sun is like a spotlight above us.

I'm surrounded by blue. Blue sky. Blue lake. "Wow," I murmur.

The lake ripples with sunlight that stretches from one end to the other. There are a few trees perched by one edge of the lake, but otherwise wildflowers are free to grow across grassy flats—and they do. Reds. Yellows. Purples. They smell so sweet I can almost taste them. There's a trail leading up the mountain beyond the lake, and more flowers climb the ridge right along with it. Patches of snow cling to the upper slopes.

Sam drops my hand and pulls off his backpack. A second later he has his camera out.

"Wait—I thought you only like to take pictures of dark and depressing things?"

"Maybe I'm feeling optimistic."

My stomach is suddenly queasy. "Sam—"

"Quiet. You're ruining the light."

Of course that makes no sense, but he's right. I'm ruining something. Why can't we have a minute here just to drink it all in like everyone else is doing? I'm quiet as he crouches, snapping pictures from low angles and then high. His hands seem too big and too rough to hold a camera so delicately. I remember how his hands felt holding me. How I felt.

"Did you get some good ones?"

"The light isn't great." He flips through his camera. "But yeah." He tilts the viewfinder so I can see as he scrolls through the shots. I don't have to stand quite so close, but I do anyway. "What were you going to do in New York?"

"New York *Film Academy*. They have a one-year photography program."

"Really?" I smile. "I know that school. They call themselves Light Hunters."

He slips his camera into his pack. "You were looking at the same school?"

"Just looking." I take a long breath, drinking in the blue beauty of the water. "I love photography, but it was always going to be a hobby. I'd planned to apply to business school at Cornell. Get my degree in financial management. I'm sure people will want to invest with me now, don't you think?" I turn to give him a half-smile. "At least there's that. The future I planned for myself is gone, too. It makes me feel less guilty sometimes."

He sighs and I realize I've gone and ruined everything anyway.

"How much farther?" he asks.

"About half a mile. We head around the lake and catch the trail over there. Are you starving? I can beg for some food, or maybe a splint and painkillers?"

"I'm okay," he says, shaking his head. "The only thing I need is at the top of this mountain. You ready?"

No. I'd rather stay here by water the color of happiness and a place that God hasn't deserted. I'd much rather sit on a log with Sam beside me and go nowhere at all.

Not forward.

Not backward.

"Ready," I say.

We make our way around the lake. We wave at a woman sitting with her feet in the water and a young couple taking a selfie from the top of a boulder. I'm light-headed when we finally turn our backs to the lake and face the uphill trail. It's still a long way up, and I'm not sure I want to see what's there.

"You're holding up traffic," Sam says.

We're back in the trees, a stream gurgling beside us, the muddy trail rising steeply. "I don't think I can do this."

"You remember the 'Best Of' that Mr. Dean posted on the website over spring break?" he asks.

"What?" I blink at him. How did I ever think he was brooding? He's gorgeous, even now. Especially now. His face is grimy, his chin scraped red beneath a shadow of stubble. His lips are cracked and his straight brows are dusted with dirt. I remember how I wanted to photograph

Gabe's face. How I wanted to capture every line and curve with my camera. With Sam it's different. I want to capture it all with my fingers.

With my lips.

Some part of me realizes this is exhaustion thrumming through my veins. This is the result of sharing a very emotional episode with someone and mistaking the rush of survival with something more.

But it doesn't change the way I feel.

"Grace?"

I blink again. I've been staring, I think. "Sorry. What did you say?"

"The collage of class photos."

"Yeah." I nod, wondering why he's bringing this up now. "I remember."

He nudges me forward, and I take a weary step. "What about it?"

"Did I tell you what I thought when I saw it for the first time?"

"You never told me anything. You acted as if I didn't exist."

"I did not."

"Yes, you did. Even on that first day. I've always wondered about that."

"About what?"

"I could have sworn you recognized me when you first saw me."

"Everyone knew you."

"So you did know who I was?" I stop to face him, but he gestures me forward. "Tell me," I say, and I start walking again.

I hear his steps behind me, the sound of his breath.

"Was it because of the Fund?" I ask. "Last night you said I wasn't the one to tell you to invest. Did you . . . Was that true?"

"It was true," he says. His walking stick thumps the ground, steady as a heartbeat. "I work for my mom when I can. I heard about the Fund from an office manager at one of the properties I was cleaning."

"Really? It wasn't me?"

Gruffly he says, "You want to know what I thought about the collage or not?"

I smile to myself. "You're very bossy, you know that?"

"Climbing up a rock wall with a sprained ankle will do that. Now pick up the pace."

"I can't even pick up my feet." But I manage to do it by focusing on Sam rather than my pain. Besides, he's made me curious. "So," I ask. "What did you think?"

"I was pissed."

"What did you have to be pissed about? You were the featured photo."

"I wasn't featured," he says. "You were."

"Me? Your photo was the biggest of them all."

"What'd you do? Measure it."

"Yes," I say. "With a ruler against my computer screen."

His next breath sounds more like a laugh.

"They were portraits," I say in my defense, "and yours was of some guy's shoe. A shoe," I repeat.

"It was a well-photographed shoe," he says. "It might have been a little bigger, but your photo was in the top right corner. Place of prominence."

"That's not what that means."

"Yeah, it is. And your photo was crap."

"What?" I add a gasp for good measure, but every breath is a gasp as I put one foot in front of the other. "My photo was amazing." My boots crunch through a tiny patch of old snow. I squint as I look up and see growing stretches of it along the peaks ahead of us.

"The whole thing was staged," he says. "And Mr. Dean had just gotten done lecturing about authenticity."

"It was authentic. That was a woman I saw at the Phoenix Zoo, sitting on the bench exactly where I shot her. I didn't hire her from Central Casting along with a zebra for the background."

"She was an old, ugly lady and you stripped her of that and made her all soft and glowy."

"Glowy?" I shoot an annoyed glance over my shoulder. "She was glowy because beauty knows no age."

"One minute while I finish puking on the side of the trail."

"Ha!" I scoff. "You want everything dark and twisted. Admit it."

"I want everything to be real. You created the image of that woman by manipulating the light."

"That's what photography is. A manipulation of light."
I balance myself at the top of a small ridge and reach down
a hand. Sam takes it, gripping my wrist with his and I hold
tight as he skips his way up.

"Yeah, and you can use light to reveal or you can use it
to trick people."

"You think she was a trick?"

"She had a chin mole with no hair."

"What?"

"Every chin mole on every eighty-year-old woman has
a hair. In your photo, you screwed with the light so she
didn't have one."

"Maybe she plucks."

"That woman hadn't seen a pair of tweezers since the
fifties."

"That's why you gave me a D on my peer review? Because of a chin hair? Do you have any idea how much I
hated you for that?"

"I had an idea." He tilts his chin, gesturing to whatever
is over my right shoulder. "Look at that."

I turn, and I'm shocked to see another lake spread before us like a deep blue carpet. "Wow."

"Guessing that's the middle lake."

"We already climbed a quarter mile?" I glance at him,
narrowing my eyes. "You were distracting me, weren't you?"

"Did it work?"

"You could've picked something nicer," I grumble.

"Then we'll talk about my photos on the next part."

"Idiot," I say. I smile even though it makes my lips crack. Even though I shouldn't let myself feel this way about a person who will remember in a quarter mile that he hates me.

Unless.

I turn away, shielding my eyes as I look up and find the clouds close enough to touch. "Just a little farther." The pain is now a part of my feet and my knees and my thighs and my back.

One. Two. Three. My mind counts with every step.

Seventeen. Eighteen. Nineteen.

I lose count and start again. And again. Until I hear Sam's voice behind me. "Grace, look! There it is."

Stopping, I lift my gaze from the trail. To our right, Upper Blue Lake rests in a small valley surrounded by snow-covered hills. But Sam isn't pointing to the lake. He's pointing to a meadow that stretches toward a cliff wall. Below it is the dark blue of the middle lake.

And a cairn of boulders as tall as a person.

"It exists!" He whoops, the sound echoing over the hills. "She was here. She didn't lie."

Hope unfurls inside me. I feel like I've grown wings and I could fly. Then Sam takes my hand. I weave my fingers with his and a sense of connection runs through me like adrenaline.

I feel like I'm part of a paper chain again.

47

August

It's spectacular up here, just like I read. The kind of beauty that steals whatever breath you have left and you don't even care.

A stripe of gold trail weaves through grassy green meadows dotted with boulders and yellow wildflowers. The lake is a glassy oval so smooth that it reflects the white clouds like they've been painted on the surface. My gaze follows the dark ridgeline to a sapphire sky. It really looks like that, too. It's perfect . . . or it would be if not for the cairn.

My pulse starts to race.

What if it's here?

What if it isn't?

"You ready?" Sam asks. His fingers squeeze mine.

I squeeze back. "No."

Our hands separate and he starts for the cairn. I follow more slowly while everything rushes back at me: Mom telling Barry that I'm the light. Mom warning me that we needed more investors. Mr. Dean wondering how to pay for his wife's dialysis. Gabe handing back my lens. Charlie saying that Bernie Madoff's son killed himself. Cecily's hand stinging hard against my cheek.

Sam.

He's standing by the pile of stones and watching me. His smile has faded and his expression is wary. He's remembered exactly who I am, too. "You want me to do it?" he asks.

I nod. There are dark specks of people on the trail above the lake, but it's just the two of us here. The wind is sharper above the tree line and cold as it comes off the water. I let my backpack slip to the dirt and tug the collar of my coat around my neck. Sam sets his pack down beside mine and shifts his weight, limping to the wall of the cairn. He circles, looking for an opening big enough for his hand. He tugs a small boulder loose and tosses it into the meadow.

"Is there . . . Can you see anything?"

"It's deeper than I expected," he says. "Hard to see without the sun overhead, but there are pockets between the boulders and maybe an open space toward the bottom." He loosens another boulder and then another, pulling down what someone carefully put up.

Each beat of my heart feels like a hammer against my temple. "Sam?"

The circle of rocks is only a few feet high now. He's bent over reaching in for something. When he pulls his hands clear, he's holding something big.

A boulder.

Disappointed, he tosses it to his side and dust floats up. I wobble back, just as weightless. "It's not there, is it?"

"It is. It has to be." He reaches back in. He heaves out another boulder, and then another. The fourth time, his grunt of effort turns into a scream of frustration.

It's not there.

I turn toward the cliff edge and look down. The face is curved inward, and I wonder if the lake was once high enough to eat away at the rock. Boulders are stacked below, huge and gray, with bits of grass growing in between. Toward the bottom of the cliff, another meadow stretches to the middle lake. It isn't fair. Not when I wanted to believe so much.

I hear Sam continuing to dig in the well of the crevice. When I turn, he's got a heavy ball of dirt in his hand. He throws it and it breaks apart against the rock. It's our futures, showering down in a cloud of dust.

My heart squeezes. It was hard enough before, but now the guilt and the pain grow to fill all the space left where I'd been holding tight to hope. I wasn't going to care about anyone, but I messed that up, too. I care about Sam. I can't stand to see him broken like this.

Like me.

Because of me.

The sky stretches toward the horizon, a watercolor of blue bleeding into white. What a pretty backdrop. But for what? I look down again and the boulders stare up at me like a mouthful of jagged teeth. It makes me think of a photo I once saw. It won a photography contest, though I don't remember which one. It was of a girl lying half on the ledge of a mountain with boulders just like these below. Her arms were spread wide in the air; the only thing keeping her up seemed to be the strength of her abs. The scenery is stunning but what makes the photo unique is the element of danger. The precipice. The way she's so close to death.

That photo won with just the hint of death.

An idea forms. Maybe there is a way to redeem myself. A way for Sam to find his own redemption.

"The student photo contest," I say suddenly.

Sam stops digging and turns to look at me. "What?"

"There wasn't much of a cash prize for the winners."

"So?" He wipes a hand across his forehead. "Help me look."

"There are other student contests, though. I used to surf through them online to see what was being submitted. Some of them give big prizes." I study the horizon, the slant of light from the west, the angle looking down into the canyon. Not ideal, but the clouds are actually really nice. "One contest pays twenty-five thousand dollars. Did you know that?" I step closer to the edge. "You just have to have the right photo. Something . . . dramatic." It's strange to watch him freeze, muscle by muscle. To have him realize what I've only just realized myself. "You should get out your camera."

"Grace," he says again. His voice is hoarse. "You promised me."

"This is different. This will mean something."

I edge closer to the cliff. My heart has expanded now to fill my chest, my throat, my mouth. It's beating along the line of my jaw and into my ear. "You wouldn't have to wait for a contest. You could sell the picture. I'm sure one of the tabloids would want it. Janelle Pierce's daughter at the very end."

"Grace—"

"You could pretend shock. You were taking my photo and I just . . . stepped off. No one would have to know."

Dirt rains from his hand, his fingers pressing the clump of packed dirt he's still holding.

"I could do something good, Sam. Make one thing right." Tears fill my eyes. "I could still be Galadriel."

"No!" he cries. "I don't care about the money."

"You do—"

"Not anymore! Not . . . Jesus, Grace. I care about you."

I shake my head, because how can that be true? "Even my own mother didn't care about me."

He steps closer and I step back. Rock crumbles behind my ankle. "Get out your camera, Sam."

"She didn't lie to you, Grace."

The wind calls me back to the edge. "The plane ticket is proof. The false passport. The empty cairn."

"Damn it, Grace. Look around." His voice is so sharp it pulls my thoughts back.

"What?"

"Just look at this place. What did she say—half a step from heaven? And it is. It is."

Clouds seem to respond, floating white on blue.

He steps closer. "Someone could have moved the bottle. It could have broken in the last freeze. The snowmelt could have taken it away."

But there's no explanation, no way to rationalize the truth. "I always loved her even when I hated her. How could I love a person who did the things she did?"

"Because you're good. Because sometimes the people we love let us down. Sometimes we let them down." His voice cracks and I'm too full of pain. I can't stand to hear his.

"You didn't," I say. "You didn't let Marcus down. You can't blame yourself."

"Part of me knows that," he says. "But part of me wishes I could go back and pour my own damn milk." He blinks hard, his jaw clenching and unclenching. "Here's the truth: We can't fix things or change them. Not the way we want. All we do is live it over and over until we're not living at all."

"So what do we do? How do we go back?"

"I don't know," he says. He looks down at the lump of dirt still in his hands and lets it drop to the ground. "Maybe that's the problem. Maybe we have to stop going back."

Shaking my head, I look beyond the precipice. The world stretches before me, a blanket of greens and browns and blues. Snowy peaks and limitless sky beyond that. "How is it possible," I say, "that I can see forever from here, but I can't see how to move on?"

I hold up my fingers, creating a frame the way I've done so many times before. I face the horizon and everywhere the world is beautiful. But it's also flat—like a painting. I think that's what the world is for us: a backdrop. For who we are. But who am I? How do I see myself as part of it when my entire life has been a lie?

"What do you see?" he asks.

"Nothing good."

"You never did know how to frame a shot." His hands rise to my shoulders and he slowly turns me toward him until he's in the middle of my frame. "What do you see now?"

Emotion wells up, filling my throat.

His expression is uncertain, but he holds my gaze. "Maybe the thing is not which direction we go from here. Maybe it's just that we don't go alone."

When the tears start, he pulls me to his chest. I close my eyes and hold on. I wish I could stay here forever. Nameless. Faceless. Shaped only by the feel of Sam's arms around me and the press of his lips in my hair.

48

August

We stand there for minutes that I wish could stretch into hours. Into days. Into forever.

But even my tears can only fall for so long, and as reality filters back into my exhausted mind, I realize I've soaked at least half of his shirt. My nose is running, too. *Oh God.* Why can't this be a movie where the scene fades to black and we reappear showered and sipping hot cocoa in front of a fire? Instead, we're filthy and the breeze has picked up. Or maybe it's that the sun has slid farther to the west. I'm still pressed to Sam's chest, but it's because my cheek is wet and sticky against him.

Embarrassed, I detach myself, wiping my face. "Sorry."

He shifts awkwardly on his bad foot. "I think my good leg fell asleep."

Our eyes meet. His lips twitch and an answering laugh bubbles up inside of me from I don't know where. But it feels good to let it out, to hear his laugh mix with mine until my eyes start to leak again.

"Please no," he says with a groan. "No more tears. My shirt can't take it." But his eyes are soft and his grin sweet as he reaches for my hand again. Together we limp and hobble our way back to the stack of boulders. Clumps of dirt dot the surface from Sam's excavation and he brushes enough aside so that we can sit next to each other.

"How are you going to make it down on that ankle?" I ask.

"Slowly."

"I could make a sled and drag you down," I offer.

He shoots me a look that says exactly what he thinks of that idea. It makes me smile even more.

"I just need a few minutes. And maybe fifteen more granola bars. Don't suppose you've been holding out on me?"

"I wish." My stomach rumbles, reminding me that I haven't had anything to eat either since the trail mix last night.

He pulls out his water bottle and there's still an inch or two of liquid left. He takes a drink and then hands it to me. I fill my mouth, swirling the water around and then hand it back. We have to go down. I know we do.

My mom is waiting.

His mom is waiting.

"Will you tell me how you captured those images?"

"Now?" But he reaches for his backpack and pulls out a camera. It's not the same one he had out earlier. This one is a Nikon but instead of an actual lens, there's a lens cap taped over the opening.

I turn it over in my hands. "What is this?" There's something familiar about it . . . and then understanding slides into place like one of Mom's puzzle boxes. "You've poked a tiny hole in the plastic, haven't you?" I grin at him. "A camera obscura."

"Technically, a pinhole camera."

We learned about them in class. I can vaguely picture a black-and-white image of a box with a hole in one end. Light streamed through the hole and created an image on the opposite wall of the box. It was how photography was invented. "You must need really long exposure times."

"Depends on the light," he says. "At least four seconds."

I look through the viewfinder at the slope of trees beside us. "What made you think of a pinhole camera?"

"You," he says.

Surprised, I lower the camera. "Me?"

"You always had the best equipment—stuff I could never afford—and I guess it pissed me off. So I decided to see how cheap I could go. Came up with the idea of a pinhole camera after reading about them online. I found a cap on eBay and started experimenting."

"I still don't get how you make people disappear."

"It was an accident the first time. I was practicing on stationary objects so I could work out the exposure times. But I wanted to try it with people. I did some selfies with a timer but they felt flat. So I took the camera to a park one day. There's a guy who sleeps there in the afternoons. He's always on a bench by the tennis courts. But when I got to the park, I saw another guy sitting on a blanket. He reminded me of Marcus. He was only a couple years older, same wavy dark hair and a LeBron jersey just like the one Marcus had. He also had a baby. A two-year-old—something like that." He smiles. "Kid was gnawing on a Nerf football. That made me think of Marcus, too. So I set up the camera, focusing on the baby. About two seconds after I hit the button, the baby dropped down to his hands and knees and crawled off the blanket. When I checked the image, the hairs on the back of my neck stood up. The baby was there, and not there."

"Like Marcus."

He nods. "Like Marcus."

I inhale deeply and let it out slowly. Blame, I think, is like the carbon monoxide in the air: if you keep breathing it in, eventually it will kill you. "Will you take my picture?"

He takes the camera back. "I don't have a tripod. It'll be blurry."

"It's okay." I move back a few steps.

"Grace, no."

"Please."

"No!" He puts the camera in his pack and zips it closed.

"It's just a picture," I say, hurt.

His eyes flicker to mine. "I don't want to make you disappear."

My heart squeezes and then expands. "I don't want

to disappear either." I sit beside him. When my shoulder touches his, he doesn't pull away.

"I'd seen a picture of you," he says. "I was working crew for my mom one night, cleaning a floor of financial offices. I saw your picture on a cover of a brochure."

"That's why you recognized me the first day of school?"

He nods. "In the photo, your face was upturned like you could see something I didn't."

I know exactly the one he's thinking of. "'Look to the future,'" I say, mimicking Barry and his prompts.

"But it made me want to. So I Googled your name and found more pictures. You were . . . beautiful. You are."

I flush. "You were so cold to me."

"Because I didn't like the way you made me feel." His voice drops. "I'd gotten good at not feeling much of anything." He reaches for a clump of dirt, nervously working it through his fingers. "You were so optimistic. You brought pictures of flowers into class, for God's sake. Stupid flowers that reminded me I'd been living without any . . . color. You made me want to be who I was. Before Marcus died."

He lifts his face to look at me. His gaze shifts from my eyes to my mouth.

When I lean toward him, he drops the clump of dirt and slides his hand up my neck and into my hair. His thumb strokes the hinge of my jaw, massaging until my mouth opens. Then he tilts his head and he kisses me.

The eggshell of my heart cracks open. I feel loose and runny inside. My hands rise to his face and I touch him the way I've been wanting to. I slide my thumbs over the curve of his cheek and line of his jaw. With my fingertips, I touch his lips where they're touching mine, where we're connected. I want to feel everything, and I feel like I'll explode if I do.

When he pulls back, I'm dizzy. I don't even try telling myself it's just the elevation. It's Sam. It's crazy and it's impossible, but it's Sam.

He rests his forehead against mine. For once, he sounds as breathless as I do. We stay that way for a long moment. When my breath is nearly back to normal, his suddenly hitches.

"Grace." His voice is choked, his muscles stiffening even as he pulls away.

"What?" My heart kicks high again, but not in a good way. "What's wrong?"

He points to the ground. For a second, that's all I see. Ground. Packed earth. Scattered bits of dust and rock. The clump of dirt Sam had been holding. Then he reaches for it and his thumb slides over the surface where something in the rock is glittering. A vein of sand in the granite, maybe. But it isn't sand. As he works more of the dirt free, it's obvious that it isn't rock at all.

It's glass.

49

August

Sam tears down every rock of the cairn. On hands and knees, I sift through every inch of dirt. We walk the surrounding ground for more glass.

For a photo impossibly preserved against snow and rain.

For a clue to where forty-five million dollars is hidden.

There's nothing.

There's just this. My fingers skim the surface—the glass is about the size of a business card, but thick and heavy and flat enough that it couldn't come from a soda bottle or something like that. More like a container. Or a jar.

"It isn't proof," I say.

He sits beside me. "I'm pretty sure it is."

I rub away more of the dirt until I can see the bubbled shine of glass. "It isn't your money."

"It'll turn up. Eventually."

I sigh. "Is it pathetic that I still want to believe? After

everything she did. The suffering she caused my friends. My family. You."

It must look like I'm going to cry again, because he pulls me to his chest. His shirt is still damp, but I don't care. I fit my face to the hollow at the base of his neck.

"Maybe it's like in photography," he says. "You can't capture light without darkness. Or darkness without light. They don't . . . exist apart from each other. Maybe it's that way with people, too."

The glass in my hand glimmers light and then dark as I shift it in and out of the lowering rays of sun. I squeeze the glass, the edges long since smoothed by the wear of time.

"Shadow and light."

50

August

We make our way down slowly, following the unhurried pace of the sun as it sinks the trail into shadow and turns the yellow leaves to green and the rock from creamy gray to smoke. It takes us nearly two hours, and I know Sam's ankle must be getting worse, because he uses his walking stick and the heel of his good shoe to skid down the steepest switchbacks. Our only conversation comes in the form of glances and smiles, though those become fewer as we get closer to the bottom. The birds appear to take our silence as an invitation to squawk from every tree limb. I don't know if they were so noisy on the way up or if I was lost in my own world.

A world that I wish I could keep at bay.

The piece of glass is still in my pocket, an awkward but comforting shape I feel with each downhill step. I'll bring it with me to the hospital tomorrow. I'll hold it when the doctors take my mother off life support. And I'll choose to believe it means she loved me.

And then?

I still don't know. In some ways, everything has changed. In some ways, nothing has.

It's fully dusk when we finally spot the logbook and then the nearly empty parking lot. We have no phone, but I can try hitchhiking again. We haven't even reached the water spigot to refill our bottles when a couple with gray hair and a dog the size of a loaf of bread notices Sam's leg. They ask if we need help. The woman is a dermatologist, and though sprained ankles aren't her specialty, she insists on wrapping his foot and cleaning out the scrapes. She replaces the bandana with bandages from her first-aid kit. When they find out we have no way back to town, they offer us a ride to Montrose, a town that's bigger than Ridgway and has its own bus station. And an airport.

I won't make it home by tomorrow at one—not by bus. But there's a late flight to Phoenix that I can still catch. My stomach drops when the man at the ticket counter tells us a one-way fare is $424.

In the end, Sam buys me a plane ticket with an emergency Visa his mother gave him after Marcus died. He covers the cost that I can't. "I'll take the bus," he says.

The whole process leaves me feeling awkward. And guilty. Under the harsh artificial lights of the small airport, my shame is back.

"I'll repay you," I mumble. We're standing by security,

the TSA employee a silent watcher, bored and ready for me to move through. Move on.

Sam hands me the ticket. "Add it to my tab." He manufactures a half-smile. He means it as a joke, but the words are a reminder of what's waiting for us at home.

My mother.

His.

The truth of what I knew.

The burden of what he lost.

A reminder of all the reasons *we* could never be *us*.

So his words become new bricks and I stack them between us, rebuilding my fortress.

"I'll see you . . . in Phoenix," he says.

And just like that, I'm back to being alone.

As I fly home, my eyes closed and my face pressed to the window, I hear his good-bye echoing over and over. I hear the pause in the middle. What had he meant to say? *Around? Soon?* Or another one of the things people say when they mean they won't see you at all.

I wonder if it's possible to live without walls, or if we can't help ourselves. If self-preservation is so strong that we push others away even when we most want to bring them close.

51

August

Uncle David picks me up from the airport. He doesn't comment on my appearance.

Or my disappearance.

He studies me for a long moment as I slide in beside him and set my backpack on the floor mat. "Did you find it?"

"What?" I ask.

"The note you left. It said you were looking for something."

I've never seen my uncle so tired. Even his eyes seem drained of color. My note—well, it wasn't much of a note, I realize.

Back in a few days. There's something I need to find.

At the least, I should have called him. He's wearing a wrinkled shirt stained with something green. I wonder if he was feeding the twins when I called.

"I'm at the airport. I don't have money for a taxi. Could you—"

"I'll be there in thirty minutes."

He was here in twenty and I wonder how many speed limits he broke. He's my only family now, and technically, he's responsible for me until I turn eighteen in a few months. But I was angry at him. I wanted to punish him for not believing. I cut him out of my life and my future using silence as my weapon.

I can feel how easy it would be to slip back into that now. How I could just turn my face to the window . . .

My hand slides to the ridge of glass in my front pocket. But it's Sam's face that comes to mind. I'm not going to go back. I'm not going to let these past few days leave me unchanged. No matter what happens, he taught me something. The mountain taught me something.

I shift in the seat until I'm facing Uncle David. "Yeah," I say. "I found what I was looking for." I swallow. "I'm sorry. For everything."

He nods. "I'm sorry, too." His eyes are suddenly wet. "Aunt Caroline and the girls are waiting. Let's go home."

52

August

My mother dies at 6:54 the next morning. The hospital calls, waking up Uncle David, who comes to wake me. But I wasn't asleep and as soon as I heard the phone, I knew.

Somehow, my mother found a way to die while on life support.

I'm numb on the way to the hospital.

I let Uncle David lead me to a waiting area. There are things happening—I don't know what. Things to do with death, I suppose. We've given permission for Donor Services to take whatever they can use, but that won't happen until later. Still, it seems like a long time passes until Uncle David comes back and asks if I want to see her.

"Grace," he asks when I don't move. "Do you want to say good-bye?"

I find myself in her room. She's lying on a pillow covered with a blanket the way I've seen her so many times over the past months. It's strange to tell myself that she's gone. Really gone this time.

I hold my breath, waiting for a deluge of pain. I expect to sink to my knees and weep like in the movies. But my eyes have chosen now to become dry. This is my mother. The only mother I will ever have, and I want to cry because then it will make us normal. We'll be the mother and daughter I always thought we were. It's not right for me to hate her.

But I do. I hate her so much because I loved her so much.

Once, my mother gave a eulogy. She told me the trick to delivering a good one was to tell a story. To remind people of the best things about the person they've lost.

What story do I tell?

What story isn't tainted by the things I now know?

I pull the piece of glass from my purse. "I found this," I tell Mom. "Up on Blue Lakes." I take a long, shuddering breath. "It was beautiful up there. You were right about that. I went there so I could find the jar you left and I could prove to myself that at least some of it was real."

Finally the tears come. Maybe I'm weak and I'm stupid. Maybe I've been played like everyone else who fell under my mother's spell. I don't know. I'll never know. I climbed that mountain so I could reach the top and see inside of her heart.

But maybe what matters is what I feel in my own.

Because my love was good.

And honest.

And true.

How can I hate myself for that?

"Good-bye, Mom," I whisper. "I'll think of you up there. I'll think of you half a step from heaven."

53

August

When we pull into the driveway at Uncle David's house—
my house—there's someone standing in the shade of the
jacaranda tree, holding a camera.

"For God's sake," Uncle David mutters. "Not all this
again."

"It's okay," I say. My heart is yo-yoing between my stomach and my throat. "I know him. He's . . . a friend."

Uncle David pulls the car into the garage and I wait
until he's inside the house before I walk back into the sun.
Sam looks as if he hasn't slept but he's showered, his hair
still damp. He's wearing shorts and there's an Ace bandage
peeking from the top of his right tennis shoe. His camera is resting against the black cotton of a T-shirt. A short-
sleeved one.

"Hi," I say, squinting up at him. "How did you find me?"

"I'm a professional stalker, remember?"

"Right." I glance at his camera and the taped-up pinhole lens.

"I was taking pictures. While I waited."

"How long have you been here?" But I think of a better question before he can answer. "How did you get here so fast from Colorado?"

"I got a ride from a truck driver in Montrose. He took me to Vegas and from there it was easy to catch an early bus. Your aunt said you'd already left for the hospital. Is your mom . . . ?"

"She died this morning. Her heart stopped—complications from pneumonia."

His eyes widen. "So you didn't . . . ?"

"I didn't."

He lets out a breath, and his shoulders seem to drop five inches. "I didn't want you to have to . . . I didn't want you to be alone."

"I wasn't. My uncle was with me."

He nods. Runs a hand through his hair. "I should have flown home with you. It wasn't right."

"It's okay," I say quickly. "You were pretty wonderful, actually. Buying me a ticket after everything that happened."

He limps deeper into the shade of the tree, his face turned away. "What happened up at Blue Lakes . . . the whole thing was crazy. Me following you. Getting lost. The storm." He turns toward me again, resting one hand on the smooth trunk. "It started to feel . . . I don't know . . ."

"Like a dream?"

He nods. "We were both exhausted. Stressed out. We said things. Did things."

His face is pinched, his gaze focused on the toe of his black Nike sneaker. My heart squeezes into a protective ball, because I know what he's about to say. I say it for him. "You mean things that you regret now."

His eyes flicker up to mine and then hold. His irises are a heat lamp that's slowly growing in strength. In warmth. Slowly drawing me in. "Things I should regret," he says. "Things I thought I'd regret."

There's a flutter in my chest that feels like my heart doubling in size, pressing against my ribs. "Like the bear," I say.

His lips curve, but it's his eyes that really smile. "Definitely the bear." He gestures to his right leg. "The sprained ankle wasn't any fun, either."

"How is it?" I ask.

"Swollen. Purple."

"My hand is scraped up pretty badly." I hold it up, though there's nothing much to see. "It hurts worse than it looks. And there are bruises on my back from one of the falls I took, and my lips are so chapped they keep cracking."

His gaze lowers to my mouth. My breath catches. "Don't forget about Dandy the dog."

"Yeah." The word is a whisper. "I do regret that." I can't take my eyes off the bow of his top lip.

He moves closer, so close it feels like we're sharing the same breath. "That scrape along your jaw." His finger strokes the length of the cut. Shivers follow his touch through every part of me. I'm dizzy with the smell of cinnamon, soap, and the memory of aspen trees.

"Then there was the kiss," he murmurs.

"Right," I say. "The kiss."

"Maybe I should regret that, but I don't."

My gaze lifts to connect with his. "I don't regret it either."

A smile transforms his face, the strength of it too powerful for any simple wall of bricks.

His hands slide into my hair, circling my ears and cradling my face. I'm sparking light like a prism. My eyes close and our lips fit together, our tongues brushing . . . my eyes wet because the way I feel is too big to hold inside.

When the kiss breaks off, he rests his forehead against mine the way he did on the mountain. "That's even better than I remembered."

I smile as his fingers slide under the sleeves of my shirt to hold my shoulders close. I do the same, running my hands up his arms, feeling the patch of bumps on his right. "You're in short sleeves."

"Yeah, well." I feel his shrug under my fingers.

My smile spreads. "I'm glad you're here."

"I shouldn't have left you at the airport. I got nervous, I guess. I'd gotten so good at being alone." His sigh is warm against my cheek. "And it was hard to trust what happened. You know? I went up that mountain expecting to find one thing, and—"

His words suddenly remind me. I pull back, startling him—startling both of us, I guess. But this is too important to wait. "I have something for you."

"For me?"

"Wait here, okay?"

He nods, still puzzled as I run into the house. When I come back outside, he's sitting under the tree, his legs stretched out. I kneel beside him and hold out my camera bag. "Take it."

"Your bag?"

"The camera. The body is smashed, but it's new and it's insured. The paperwork is in one of the inner pockets. You can get a replacement. Plus, the long lens isn't damaged and you can get six hundred dollars for it online. I checked."

He turns the bag over in his arms. "We should turn this in to the FBI."

"But it's rightfully yours. It's enough to get you started in New York."

"Yeah, but—"

"I know how much you want to leave town—to start again."

He fiddles with the zipper. "I never did take the GED this summer. I figured I might stick around and finish high school the old-fashioned way."

"Really?" I try to sound matter-of-fact, even though my pulse is jumping.

"My mom's going to start looking for a buyer for the

business. She thinks a year will give her enough time to get a good price for her client list, and she can also be researching where to set up near my aunt."

"So she's okay, then?"

He nods. "She's like you. Keeps trying to find the good in everything. Even her son." He finally unzips the bag and pulls out the new lens. He turns it in his hands. His gaze is distant, though, and I wonder if he's taking a last look at a future he won't have.

"You look so sad," I say.

"I'm not." He carefully replaces the lens, zips up the bag, and hands it back. "I'm surprised. I wanted to get away. Now I can't believe how much I want to stay." His gaze finds mine again. "Crazy as that sounds."

"Someone once said there's a thin line between crazy and creative."

He grins in a way I'm already starting to love. "So maybe we could hang out? Without the bears and blood and hypothermia?"

"Spoilsport," I tease.

I settle beside him so our shoulders are touching.

"I was thinking I would go back to school, too," I say. "I was going to do it online, but I'd be alone so much, and there's a pretty good school near here."

"Cactus High." He nods. "We played them in football."

"And then," I say, "college. It's a lot to think about, but I have options." I wrap my arms around my bent knees. "Uncle David spoke with the FBI. They'll keep searching for more clues, but Donovan said he'll respect my privacy. He wants me to get out from under this—that's what he told my uncle."

"You didn't do anything wrong, Grace. Nothing the rest of us wouldn't have done for our families."

"I wish I felt that way, but I'm working on it." I smile and change the subject. "You going back to Desert Sky?"

"That's the plan. Coach Abrams has been wanting to help me since Marcus died. He had this idea last year that I think I might say yes to."

"What idea?"

"It's embarrassing."

That makes me grin. "Tell me."

"He runs Pee Wee Football leagues. He says the parents go nuts for pictures. He wants to introduce me as the team photographer and arrange a picture day for the kids. I get candid shots during the games and they can order them online. All I need to do is create a website."

I laugh at the thought. Sam at Pee Wee Football games. I can't imagine anything more adorable, though I don't think he'd like that description.

Then I catch a strange look on his face and my laughter fades. "What?"

"I like your laugh. I liked hearing you laugh on the mountain." His eyes glimmer. "I'm not so sure I like it *now*."

I laugh again and wrap my hands around his arm to squeeze. "Mr. Roadkill is going to be taking pictures of kids playing football. How cute is that? You could sell merchandise, too. Picture mugs and picture T-shirts and picture—"

"I knew I shouldn't have told you."

My laughter dies down and then our smiles fade into quiet. But it's a peaceful quiet. He covers my hand with his—and the connection is infinitely sweet. No more walls. This is what I want to build on—this feeling inside of me right now.

I let the day settle over me. The heat, and the stillness, and the limitless sky. I squeeze Sam's arm, and he squeezes back.

Things won't be easy. I know that. The shadow of what's happened is still there. But I also know that if you can see a shadow, it's because there's light beyond it.

ACKNOWLEDGMENTS

Writing a novel is never easy, but *The Fall of Grace* was especially difficult. The story itself fought me every step of the way (and there were a lot of steps up that mountain)! It also led me into areas I knew nothing about—financial fraud, FBI investigations, photography, medical emergencies—so I needed a lot of help. I'm hugely blessed to have a wide network of accomplished friends who, if they don't know the answers, know someone who does. A heartfelt thank-you to the following who shared their time and expertise: Kevin Rapp, Assistant US Attorney, Financial Crimes Section; Brad Lemon, financial advisor; Sean McElenney, lawyer; and LeAnn Dykstra, who has become my go-to nurse. Any factual errors are entirely mine.

There were many times when I wanted to put this book down. (Or throw it.) (Or burn it.) I stuck with it, thanks to the help of these talented people who read all or part of this novel: Terry Lynn Johnson, Christina Mandelski, Gae Polisner, Erin Jade Lange, Bill Konigsberg, and Bethany Neal. A special thanks to my agent, Caryn Wiseman. I'm not sure how it's possible to hold someone's hand over the phone, but she did.

Thank you to the team at Delacorte and especially to Krista Vitola. As always, her input made the book so much stronger. And to Monica Jean, who took over this project with capable and caring hands—thank you for helping to usher Grace into the world.

A shout-out to everyone who encourages and supports me—librarians, teachers, bloggers, readers—you all keep me afloat. And to my Ahwatukee friends, who are like family, and to my family, who I would be lost without: Rachel, Kyle, and Jake.

ABOUT THE AUTHOR

AMY FELLNER DOMINY loves writing for kids of every age. She's the author of picture books as well as middle-grade novels and young adult novels, including *The Fall of Grace, Die for You, A Matter of Heart,* and *OyMG,* a Sydney Taylor Notable Book. Amy lives with her family in Phoenix. To learn more about Amy and her books, visit her online at amydominy.com or follow @amydominy on Twitter.